A MAN CALLED JUSTICE

JOHN DEACON

Cover design by German Creative on Fiverr

Edited by Karen Bennett

Want to know when my next book is released? SIGN UP HERE.

❀ Created with Vellum

For my wife, Christina, with all my love.

CHAPTER 1

1883
New Mexico Territory

Thundering hooves pounded closer, the approaching riders whooping like a bunch of wild savages.

Despite the heat of the day, their laughter chilled Nora Eckert's blood. For life had taught her a particularly hard truth: no sound in the world, not even the roar of a grizzly, is so dangerous the laughter of wicked men.

"Hush, Eli," she whispered. "We have to hide."

Nora's heart pounded as she waded into the river and pulled her six-year-old son into a tall stand of bulrushes.

She watched with growing terror as four riders came into view, a rough and dusty lot with tied-down pistols. Laughing coarsely, they dismounted not a hundred feet away.

As their horses drank, the men passed a bottle, talking loudly.

"This is as good a place as any," said the biggest of the men, a surly looking redhead Nora didn't recognize.

She held Eli close with one arm, praying the men would not discover them.

In her free hand, she clutched Blake's Remington New Model Army revolver, carefully keeping the heavy old pistol out of the water. If it came to gunplay, Nora knew she and Eli would not survive, but she vowed to kill at least one outlaw, maybe two, before they ended her.

Perhaps these men were just drunk and rowdy. Perhaps they weren't as bad as she feared.

The beefy redhead nodded toward a dusty lump he had apparently been dragging behind his horse and said something Nora couldn't hear.

One of the men walked over and kicked the lump.

The lump groaned.

Nora's blood froze.

The lump was a person. A man.

They had been dragging a living man behind their horses, dragging him over the hard ground, over sand and stone and cactus and Lord knew what else.

What manner of scoundrels would do such a thing?

But you know their type, don't you, Nora? she thought, clutching the pistol of her murdered husband. *You know their type all too well.*

Two of the outlaws untied the man and lifted him from the ground. He sagged between them, a tall man covered in dust and blood. They hauled him to the center of the clearing.

The poor man. Nora wished she could help him. But there was no way. No way at all.

She could only hope to save her son and herself.

"No matter what happens, Eli," she whispered to her

trembling son, "no matter what these men do, you must not make a sound. Do you understand?"

He nodded against her, and Nora prayed fervently, first for her son, then for herself, then for the outlaws' suffering victim.

The bloody-faced man lifted his head, glared at his interrogator, and spoke in a deep voice steeped in pain. "You men will pay."

This got them to laughing again.

"Bold words for a dead man," the burly redhead said and socked the tall man in the stomach.

The tall man grunted, and his legs gave.

The laughing men held him by the arms and kept him from falling.

"Hold him up," the redhead said. "You ride in here, think you're gonna save this place, mister? Is that what you think?"

The tall man said nothing.

"You fixing to save this land?" the redhead said. "Well, let me explain something. You can't save a forsaken land. This land is past saving." To his men, the redhead said, "Cut off them rags."

Steel flashed as a man with honey-colored hair sliced through the dusty shirt of their captive. Another outlaw started tugging the rags from the tall man's battered torso.

Nora winced, seeing the terrible wounds there.

"Hold on," the redhead said. "Give me the star first."

The fourth man, a cantering hunchback whose vile grin split a beard as black as midnight, shot forward, tugged at the wounded man's chest, and handed something to the redhead.

The redhead held up the item.

Seeing what it was, Nora stifled a gasp.

The silver star shone in a shaft of light falling between the cottonwoods.

The men beat him terribly. Someone cut a switch. They

lashed him and cursed him and mocked his goodness. "Where's your almighty law and order now?"

Nora clutched Eli's face to her bosom, wishing she had two free hands to cover the boy's ears.

Through it all the tall man did not cry out.

Finally, they hoisted him into the lower branches of a cottonwood.

Initially, Nora thought they were hanging him, but then she saw that the rope encircled not his neck but his bare chest.

"Wish I had some nails," the redhead said.

"There's a ranch over yonder," the hunchback said. He nodded toward Nora's home and set her heart to galloping.

"We ain't got time for that," the redhead said. "Besides, you know what the boss said. He's gonna reason with these small timers first."

"I was just gonna get some nails," the hunchback laughed, "not burn 'em out."

"With a man like you, Beachem, one begets the other. Now stop your yapping and tie him up real tight. I want folks to see what becomes of saviors in this territory."

Laughing, the outlaws scrambled into the cottonwood. They secured the tall man's chest to the tree, stretched his arms out straight, and tied his wrists to the branches.

At a glance it appeared he had been crucified.

Again, Nora's blood ran cold.

Such evil. Such unfathomable evil.

Lord, she prayed, clutching her son, *deliver us from evil. And please, Lord, have mercy on this man. Please rescue him. If not for his sake, for ours. In a country given over to wickedness, we must have at least one good man.*

Then, as if making light of her prayers, one of the men said, "This boy's deader'n a hammer, Del Mundo."

The redhead—presumably *Del Mundo*—cursed bitterly. "I figured on getting some target practice."

"Alive or dead, we can still use him as a target," Beachem the hunchback said, dropping from the tree as nimbly as a monkey.

"Where's the fun in that?" Del Mundo said. "Shooting a dead man is a waste of ammunition. Besides, there's a storm brewing. We gotta ride. Hey Tate, catch."

He flicked his wrist. A bit of color shot from his hand into the hands of the brown-haired man still perched in the tree.

"Pin that on him."

"Pin it on him? He ain't got a shirt."

"Pin it on him anyway."

Leaning over, Tate pushed the badge pin into the dead man's chest in a final mockery of his former profession.

Sickened by their cruelty, Nora felt a wild urge to open fire on the men. But doing so would get her and Eli killed.

Instead of shooting, she prayed and hugged her tiny son as the men drank more whiskey and mounted up.

Thunder grumbled.

The men rode off toward the east, hooting and hollering as they departed.

Once they were gone, Nora led her shocked son onto dry ground and released his hand.

"Stay here now, baby," she said. "Mama will be right back."

Leaving her boy hidden among the scrub, she raced across the clearing. She hiked up her dress and climbed the tree, hoping for a miracle.

"Please, Lord," she prayed aloud, "please let there have been a mistake. Let this man yet live."

But touching his cooling flesh, she felt no pulse.

Hot tears sprang from her eyes.

She would not leave him hanging here as some gruesome spectacle.

First, she unfastened his wrists. Then, undoing their knots, she strained, using the rope around his chest to lower the dead man gently to the ground.

She knelt at his side checking his throat and wrists and bare chest, avoiding the badge that Del Mundo and the others had fastened so cruelly to the tall man's flesh.

Despite her thorough investigation and heartfelt prayers, however, she still detected no pulse.

The man was dead.

She rocked back, weeping hot tears, and cried out with an agony of emotion.

The demise of this stranger brought Blake's death rushing back to her. In her mind she heard again the sound of bootheels on the porch boards, and she remembered the crumbling sensation she had felt opening the front door and seeing the Patterson brothers standing there, looking pale and sick with their hats clutched to their bellies. *Why,* she had wondered in that moment of dawning terror, *were their clothes so bloody?*

Now, dual rivers of grief and injustice poured into her, forming a confluence of pure outrage.

Nora opened her burning eyes, stared up at the stormy skies overhead, and gave voice to the tempest within her, praying hard.

The prayers themselves were also hard.

Starting with *Psalm 69*, which she had committed to memory after the murder of her husband two years earlier, she unleashed a prayer of heartfelt imprecation. "All my enemies are before you, Lord. Pour out your wrath on them; let your fierce anger overtake them."

This prayer flowed through the dark and desperate caverns of her embittered heart, crying out not only for deliverance but also for vengeance. Nora Eckert was a good and Godly woman pushed to her limit. The cruelty of this lawless frontier had ground her down, honing her spirit to a killing edge.

"How much longer, Lord? How much longer will you remain silent in the face of such evil? We hunger for righteousness, Lord. We hunger for justice!"

There was a blinding flash.

Nora tumbled backward as if pushed by an invisible hand and cried out, filled with terror, her voice lost in the booming crack of thunder.

"Mama!" Eli cried, running to her.

Nora sat up, blinking, and scuttled backward several steps staring in disbelief as smoke rose from the chest of the dead man.

Her mouth dropped open.

This was how God answered the prayers of her heart? Not by saving the dead man or punishing his killers but by striking the lawman's corpse with lightning?

She stared in disbelief at the aftermath.

The lightning had struck his badge. The silver star smoldered now, having lost a bit of definition. The metal had, she was horrified to note, melted into the flesh of the dead man. The surface of the badge had drawn even with his chest, having become a part of him.

"Oh!" she cried in sudden shock, and Eli scampered back.

"What is it, Mama?"

Nora blinked, staring in disbelief.

Had she imagined that?

No.

There it was again.

The badge continued to move, riding up and down as the chest of the man rose and fell, rose and fell.

The lightning-struck lawman had come back to life.

CHAPTER 2

He awoke to a world of pain and confusion and muffled voices. He lay atop a bed in a dim, unfamiliar room.

Everything hurt.

He blinked, accepting the pain.

Where was he?

How had he gotten here?

Why was he in pain?

And above all else… who was he?

He blinked again, examining his confusion. He felt awake and alert, but he had no memory.

Was this his home?

He turned his head in the direction of the muffled voices, which were growing clearer, and saw that he was not, after all, alone in this gloomy space.

A small boy stood beside the bed clutching a large revolver in both hands, holding it by the grip and barrel like a carbine.

The man was pleased to see the weapon was not pointed in his direction but rather at the voices beyond the curtain.

Or rather, the man soon began to suspect, the pistol was pointed at *one* of the voices beyond the curtain.

"May I fetch you a drink of water, Mr. Haversham?" a woman's voice asked. "I do apologize for not inviting you in, but sickness has struck our home. My son lays bedridden beyond that curtain."

"No thank you, Widow Eckert. I just filled my canteen. I surely hope your boy is feeling better soon."

"Thank you, Mr. Haversham. Now, I don't mean to be rude, but what is it that brings you by this day? I have a heap of work to see to."

"No doubt you do, ma'am. Please pardon my intrusion, and I promise to not take much of your precious time."

"Tucker sent you?"

"Yes, ma'am. He's wondering if you had reconsidered his offer."

"Up one side and down the other, Mr. Haversham. But my answer remains the same. I am not interested in selling the ranch."

"I understand, Widow Eckert. It's a beautiful spread, what with the mountains behind you. Handy, too, with the river right here. How many head of cattle are you running?"

"Not many at the moment."

"Thirty? Forty? A ranch this size could easily support three times that many."

"Not many at the moment," she repeated. "But we get by."

"It must be difficult for a woman being all alone out here."

"My boy is a help."

"But without a man…"

"We get by. Out here neighbors help one another. It's a way of life."

"Well, that is a heartwarming sentiment, Widow Eckert. It genuinely warms my heart. And I assure you that another of your neighbors, Mr. Tucker, also wishes to help you and your boy. In fact, Mr. Tucker has magnanimously authorized me to tack an additional 500 dollars onto his original offer."

"That's very generous of him, but please tell Mr. Tucker that I do not wish to sell at any price. I will not leave my home."

Who are these people? the man wondered, lying in the gloom. *This woman, this boy. Are they my family?*

He shifted his weight and winced at the pain.

The boy turned toward him, and his tiny mouth dropped open.

The man pointed his finger toward the muzzle now leveled on him and raised his eyebrows.

The boy, apparently only then realizing that he had inadvertently pointed the pistol at the man, quickly turned the muzzle aside. Then he lowered the revolver to his side, raised one hand to his mouth, and pressed a single finger to his pursed lips.

The man might not recognize the boy, but he understood the gesture.

Shh. Lay still and be quiet.

The man nodded.

"Yes, this territory seems like a terribly hard place for a woman all on her own," the voice of Mr. Haversham continued beyond the curtain. "All the work, the heat, the cold, the storms. And the danger? You must be quite a woman, Widow Eckert."

"I am a plain, hardworking woman, Mr. Haversham. Speaking of which—"

"Don't the dangers concern you, though?" Haversham interrupted. "Outlaws and Indians, flash floods and rattlesnakes, bears and cougars…"

"Like I said, we get by."

"Yes, for now. But I have heard tales lately of cattle rustlers harassing your neighbors."

"Are you threatening me, Mr. Haversham?"

"Threatening you? Of course not, Widow Eckert. Quite the opposite. I am only trying to help you avoid trouble."

"I'll say it again. We get by."

"Well, I am certainly glad to hear that, Widow Eckert. But sometimes, a woman gets a notion in her head, like maybe thinking she can handle a place all on her own, and she holds onto that notion even when the place is falling apart, and her herd is dwindling, and she has run up a big tab at Mueller's Mercantile. I mean, what would she do if Mr. Mueller had a change of heart and demanded she settle her debt?"

"I'm sure that would be her business and none of yours, Mr. Haversham. Now, if you'll excuse me, I need to see to my work. Please tell Mr. Tucker that I will never sell this place. That is my final answer. Good day, Mr. Haversham."

"Good day, Widow Eckert… and good luck."

After Haversham left, the man heard the door shut and latch.

The boy opened the curtain.

Light flooded the room making the man squint.

The boy looked around six or seven and had straight hair the color of straw. "Mama, he's awake!"

CHAPTER 3

"He is?" the woman said, sounding excited.

The man sat up in bed and reflexively put a hand to his ribs. He felt like he'd been trampled by stampeding buffalo.

A young, attractive woman of medium height and slender build stepped into view and took the revolver from her small son. White-blond hair framed her heart-shaped face, contrasting sharply with her bright eyes, which shone as blue as a summer sky.

Seeing him sitting there, the woman smiled.

It was a rather pretty smile, he thought, one a man would hunt for after he'd seen it even once.

"Welcome back to the world," she said. "How are you feeling?"

"Like I been drug through a knothole backwards, then skinned for good measure. Feels like my ribs are busted."

"I believe they are. Eli, fetch our guest a glass of water."

Our guest, he thought. So no, this was not his family.

"You must be powerfully thirsty," the woman said.

"Yes, ma'am," he said with a nod. Even that slight motion

hurt, but he kept it from showing. He might be laid low, might not even remember who he was or what had happened, but even in this state he understood that complaining did no good.

"I'm Nora Eckert," the woman said, stretching out her hand, "and I am so very glad to finally meet you."

He shook her hand, impressed by her firm grip. "*Finally?* How long have I been here?"

"Just shy of two weeks."

"Two weeks? I've been laying here that long?"

"Yes sir."

"You've been caring for me that whole time?"

"Yes sir, as best we could. There were times in the beginning where I wasn't sure you were going to hold on, but Praise God, you pulled through."

He nodded. "Well, thank you, ma'am. I appreciate you and Eli taking care of me, and once I'm back on my feet I will do whatever I can to repay you."

"There is no debt," Nora Eckert said. "That's what good folks do. They take care of each other."

"Are you a good man?" Eli asked, handing him a drink of water.

The man smiled and took a drink. The water was so cold it burned the back of his throat. He sputtered a little, took another sip, then downed the whole glass. "Thank you, Eli. I was so thirsty I would've drunk a bottle of sand. And to answer your question, I hope so."

"You *hope* you're a good man?" the boy asked, tilting his head like a quizzical dog.

"That's right. I hope I'm a good man. Because I'll be honest. I can't remember anything."

"What do you mean?" Nora Eckert asked with obvious concern.

The man shrugged. "Just what I said. I can't remember

anything. Not you folks, not what happened, not even where I came from or who I am."

"You don't even know your own name?" Eli asked, clearly amazed.

"No, not even my name. What can you folks tell me?"

"Eli, fetch another glass," Nora Eckert said. Then she proceeded to tell the man everything she knew, recounting the day she had taken Eli to the river and hidden when the four men came riding in.

"I died?"

"You did. But I prayed for your life and for vengeance upon these wicked men, and the good Lord brought lightning out of the sky, struck your chest, and started your heart beating again."

"Lightning struck my chest and brought me back to life?" It all sounded a bit far-fetched to him.

"Yes," Nora Eckert said. "Are you well enough to stand? I'll show you."

She held out her hand and helped him to his feet.

He staggered, but Nora moved in close and slipped an arm around his waist.

Draping one arm over her shoulders, he limped beside her. He felt weak and unstable, but Nora steadied him. Beneath his arm her body was firm with muscle built through hard work.

Nora led him across the humble yet tidy ranch house to where a mirror hung on the wall.

Staring into it he saw a square-jawed, chestnut-bearded stranger with a drawn face and bright green eyes set on either side of a crooked nose.

There was a flicker of recognition, as if he were seeing the face of an old acquaintance after many years apart. But that flicker died.

"The swelling's gone down and most of the bruises have faded," Nora said.

Eli handed the man a second glass of water. "At first, you were so beat up you looked like a purple pumpkin, mister."

"Eli," the woman said sharply. "Mind your manners."

"Yes, ma'am."

The man spared the boy half a grin, then looked in the mirror again.

What a strange moment. Like being born as an adult with no name, no past, no purpose.

Though he reckoned he did have two purposes, at least.

He meant to repay these kind folks. And he also meant to repay the men who beat him and left him for dead.

"If you'll open your shirt," Nora Eckert said, "you'll see where the lightning struck you."

He unbuttoned the shirt, which fit him well enough across the shoulders but was a tad baggy and short, he realized.

He was tall, probably two or three inches north of six feet, and his body was lean and muscular and crosshatched in scars.

These facts barely registered, however, because his gaze fastened with amazement onto his chest.

Shining from the muscle there, embedded *into* it, was a silver star.

A badge, he thought. *A partially melted badge.*

Twisting a little he studied the reflection, reading the single word that remained on the badge.

Justice.

Somehow, that lone word felt more familiar and truer to his identity than even his own face.

"The lightning hit your badge and melted it into your flesh," Nora Eckert explained. "I thought about trying to pry it loose, but I was afraid I would do more harm than good."

He nodded, now noticing the strange, purple marks stretching away from the badge through his flesh like so many tentacles—marks no doubt left by the lightning strike.

No matter how fantastic it had sounded, Nora Eckert's story was true.

"The badge is part of you now," she said. "At least there's no corruption. Those marks concerned me at first, but they are from the lightning not infection."

He nodded, accepting her words.

"Does looking in the mirror help you remember anything?" Nora asked. "Seeing your face, do you remember your name?"

He shook his head. "No," he confessed, touching the silver star, "but this'll do for now."

"What's that?"

He ran a finger underneath the single word remaining on the badge. "Call me Justice."

CHAPTER 4

Over the course of the next few weeks, Justice got to know Nora and Eli Eckert.

They were good country people, industrious and hospitable and very close to one another.

Nora Eckert was an excellent cook, especially considering how little time she had in the kitchen, given the overwhelming demands of the ranch.

Eli was bright and capable for his age. Hardworking and respectful to his mother, he nonetheless smiled easily and loved to laugh.

Despite their hard work the ranch was failing. Everywhere from the pile of unsplit oak to the sagging roof of the stable, Justice saw jobs large and small waiting.

Which made sense. How couldn't there be unfinished jobs with just this woman and her young son to do the work?

They had half a dozen cows and a young bull. Over the years since Nora's husband had died, they had sold off most of their cattle, including all their steers, to make ends meet.

Taking all this in and watching them work each day from dawn to dusk, Justice knew the Eckerts were the soul of this raw frontier, the very embodiment of faith, persistence, and decency.

Justice did what he could to help, which wasn't much at first, but with each passing day he found himself able to do more.

Unfortunately, he still remembered nothing of his previous life. But by his actions and inclinations, he and the Eckerts got to see what sort of man he was.

When he discovered that the woman and her child had been sleeping on the floor in the main room, sacrificing their bed, shame stabbed him in the heart. Immediately, he moved out of the curtained space and took up residence in the barn just a short distance from the stable that housed the Eckerts' horse, Daisy, and a pair of intelligent, cantankerous mules.

Their dog Rafer, a large, lanky mutt of many colors, attached itself immediately to Justice and followed him everywhere, even bedding down next to him at night. Rafer was smart and shaggy and mostly standoffish, despite shadowing Justice night and day. He looked to be about half wolf and acted the part convincingly.

Justice's sleep was troubled with half-formed dreams out of which leered lurid faces laughing wickedly.

Nora had told him what she knew of the men who had killed him.

The leader was a burly redhead called Del Mundo.

Another was a black-haired hunchback who never quit moving. His name was Beachem.

Then there was Tate, the brown-haired outlaw who'd pierced Justice's flesh with the badge's pin.

The final man had cut off Justice's shirt. Nora didn't know this man's name but recounted that he was young, almost as burly as Del Mundo, and had a thick blond beard and a full head of honey-colored hair.

Eventually, Justice promised himself, he would track these men down and make them pay. He did not concern himself with how, exactly, he would accomplish this. It was merely inevitable.

One way or the other he would have his vengeance.

But for the time being he needed to heal, and there was lots of work to be done.

As his condition improved, so did his stamina. He was able to work harder and longer each day. And the more he worked, the more his strength returned to him.

Four weeks after waking he felt good as new save for his ribs and his missing memory. But truth be told, the void of his past didn't bother him much. After all, you can't miss what you don't remember.

For the time being this life, taken with the knowledge of what he must one day do, was enough.

He liked the Eckerts very much. In fact, he often wished he had awakened to find himself the man of this household.

Nora Eckert was a beautiful, hardworking woman, and Eli was everything a man could want in a son.

But he was not the man of the household. That man, Blake Eckert, had died at the hands of outlaws and was buried a short distance from the ranch house.

Widowed at twenty-one Nora explained that Blake had been twenty years her senior.

Which boggled Justice's mind. Why would a woman so intelligent and beautiful marry a man old enough to be her father?

But he would not disrespect her or her deceased husband by asking for an explanation.

Besides, surveying the wide-open country surrounding the sprawling ranch, he reckoned the answer was probably right there before his very eyes.

Nora had grown up on a ranch in West Texas with very

few neighbors spread far, far apart. Seclusion sorely limited a young woman's choice of suitors.

Whatever the case Nora was a remarkable woman, and any man on the planet would be lucky to call her his wife. Justice might not remember his past, but he felt incredibly lucky for waking among these excellent people, and it was his pleasure to help them in any way he could.

He fished the river with some success, catching cutthroat trout and flathead catfish.

When he borrowed Nora's Sharps rifle and went hunting, he learned the flip side of the terrible scars that marked his body. Yes, he had been shot on a few occasions during his mysterious past, but he clearly knew how to handle firearms, too.

It was nothing for him to judge distance or make necessary adjustments according to range, and he dropped a trotting antelope at 300 yards with no problem.

This pleased him as he dressed the animal and packed it home atop one of Nora's mules, not only because he would be contributing meat to the Eckerts' table but also because he knew that eventually, he had two-legged quarry to hunt.

Soon, he thought. *Soon.*

CHAPTER 5

One day as Justice was shoring up the crumbling foundation beneath one corner of the ranch house, a lone horseman came riding up.

Watching Rafer's tail wag, Justice didn't bother heading inside to fetch the Sharps he sometimes used to hunt antelope for the Eckerts' table.

Instead, he stood, dusted himself off, and raised a hand in greeting.

The rider, a gray-haired man with a drooping mustache, lifted his hat, rode up, and introduced himself as Diego Contreras, a neighbor.

"Welcome," Justice said.

Diego dismounted with the grace of a much younger man.

They shook hands.

Diego had the grip of a rancher, that was for sure.

"You're the tallest man I've ever seen," Diego said matter-of-factly. "Where're Nora and Eli?"

"Picking berries."

"Bit early, ain't it?"

Justice nodded toward the range. "They rode over to the foothills. Berries are getting color over there."

Diego nodded. "Before you know it, it'll be snowing. So you decided to live, huh?"

"I reckoned it beat the alternative. Go ahead and let your horse drink. You want some water?"

One corner of Diego's mustache twitched. "Do I have to drink out of the trough?"

"Not unless it appeals to you," Justice said, liking this old man. "I was figuring we'd head inside and pump some instead."

"I could use a drink," Diego said. He tied his horse beside the trough, then pulled a few parcels from his saddle bags. "My wife baked bread, and I brought some venison I harvested this morning."

"Thank you," Justice said. "Nora will be pleased."

"I suppose I'll give these to you," Diego said, handing over a small bundle that gave a metallic clink as he dropped it in Justice's hand.

"Ammunition?" Justice guessed as they started for the house.

Diego nodded. "For the rifle. Last time I checked, Nora only had half a dozen cartridges left."

"We were down to half that," Justice said. "Thank you."

"I reckon you might be needing them soon. Folks been having trouble with rustlers lately."

Justice nodded grimly and slid the cartridges into his pocket. "I'll be ready. Who are they?"

"Can't say for sure, but I do have suspicions. You heard of this newcomer, Tucker?"

Justice nodded. "Sent somebody out here a couple times looking to buy Nora's place."

"That would be Haversham. Strutting, little, citified dandy?"

"I didn't see him, but yeah, that was his name, Haversham."

"He's all smiles and sneers, that one. He's the velvet glove."

"And you reckon these rustlers are Tucker's fist?"

"Makes sense, don't it? Only folks I hear getting their cattle rustled are those who've refused to sell to Tucker. Those Texas cattlemen are a tough breed. Downright ruthless, some of them. And Tucker strikes me as the type, all steers and swagger and heaven help whoever stands in his way. Know what I mean?"

"I reckon I do."

"Now, Tucker's locked down a quarter of a million acres here."

"Lot of ground."

"It is. But not when you're running 7,000 head of cattle, which is what I heard Tucker brought out of Texas. He needs more land. More grass, more water."

"Why come here then? Why leave Texas in the first place?"

"That's where the story gets downright interesting. The way I hear it, Mr. Sullivan Tucker got too big for his britches, tried grabbing land, and the other ranchers banded together and drove him out."

They went inside. Diego set the bread and meat on the counter.

Justice fetched him a glass of water, and they talked for a while, Diego explaining that his ranch abutted Nora's.

Born Mexican, Diego had become New Mexican in 1848 as part of the Treaty of Guadalupe Hidalgo. Fifteen years later he left his ranch and fought for the Union for three years. Then he'd come back and had prospered ever since, building his ranch and loving his family, which amounted to his wife and their three daughters, all of whom had grown and moved on to start families of their own.

"My story's a touch shorter," Justice said. "I don't remember anything before waking here a month ago."

Diego nodded. "All right. Guess that makes it easy to get to know you, anyway."

"There is that."

"What do you aim to do?"

"First, help out here, get Nora's ranch fixed up."

"Good. She needs the help."

Justice nodded. "Then, once she's in good shape, I have some men to track down."

"The ones who hurt you?"

"Killed me."

"Killed you, then. What do you know about them?"

Justice told him.

Then it was Diego's turn. "The only one I've heard of is the hunchback, Harvey Beachem. He's from over Cold Springs way. From what I hear he's caused all sorts of problems over there."

"How do I get to Cold Springs?"

"It's about a day's ride from here, over in the mountains. But you'd best get your strength back first, partner. Beachem's not to be trifled with. He's twitchy, quick. Killed a man in Santa Fe and another up in Leadville. Those are just the ones I know of, and it ain't like I've been asking after him. By all accounts he's got a mean streak wider than a buffalo's forehead. And wanted men are dangerous men."

"If he's wanted, why don't they just haul him in?"

Diego snorted. "You ever been to Cold Springs?"

"Your guess is as good as mine. But not that I recall."

"Well, you want to paint that town red, you wouldn't need too many buckets. You got a saloon and the mercantile and one muddy street of little shops barely hanging on. The sheriff's about a hundred and forty years old. I don't think he even wears a pistol. That's why they don't haul in Beachem.

You'd best take your shooting iron if you go to Cold Springs. Or Dos Pesos. Or anywhere in this territory, for that matter."

"Those men took everything I owned… including any and all firearms."

"Well, I might could loan you one of mine when the time comes."

"I'd be much obliged."

"But not until you get healed up."

"I'm pretty much there."

"It's the *pretty much* part that concerns me. If you get killed, Beachem keeps my gun."

Justice laughed. "All right. I'll wait a bit. Nora still needs help with a pile of work. There's wood to split and fences to mend."

Diego nodded. "And after you finish, more work will show up. Ever consider forgetting Beachem and these other men and settling into a rhythm here? Be nice for Nora and Eli, having a man here."

"It's a pleasant sentiment," Justice said, "if she'd have me. But if I forgot about Beachem and these others, I wouldn't be much of a man for Nora or Eli or even myself. Before I settle anywhere these killers will pay."

"What else do you know about them?"

Justice shrugged. "Nothing, other than what I told you."

"Tall order, tracking down unknown men in country like this. You're liable to run afoul of their type every direction you ride. It ain't like that sort's uncommon in these parts."

"I'll track them down, whatever it takes."

"Payback isn't always all it's cracked up to be."

"This isn't just about payback. Nora says they laughed while they strung me up. Beachem, these other men, they're like wild dogs. They get a taste for blood, they want more. If I don't stop them they will kill more people. They need to be put down."

CHAPTER 6

Nora stirred potatoes and onions in the hot skillet, pleased by the way the sizzling married the sound of Justice splitting wood outside. Together, these sounds created the music of a harmonious home.

In the six weeks since Justice had awakened, he had regained his full strength. And he was a strong man indeed, a man who could work from dawn till dusk without tiring. Part of his incredible stamina was due, of course, to the smooth movements of his muscular body.

He was a tall man, broad-shouldered and narrow-hipped, with long limbs corded in hard muscle. His every movement was efficient, and he worked with a graceful rhythm.

Though the badge suggested he had been a lawman, she suspected he had been a rancher at some point, too. Whatever needed fixing he spotted it, understood it, and saw it done, no requests from her necessary at all.

She hoped he would stick around for the harvest. It sure would make life easier.

And not just easier, if she was honest with herself. Better.

She loved her son more than anything in the world, but it was nice having another adult around to talk with.

It's not just that he's an adult, she told herself, and looking out the door seeing his scarred and shirtless torso ripple as he split another log, she felt heat in her face.

Justice was quite a man.

Strong, hardworking, intelligent, and calm. He was good with the animals. He understood cattle and handled a horse better than anyone she'd ever seen. Even the mule listened to him. The dog, half-wild creature that he was, nonetheless followed Justice everywhere.

And not just the animals loved him.

Nora frowned, dreading the moment Justice would announce his departure. It would break Eli's heart.

The boy was so grown up for his years, she sometimes forgot he was only six.

Over these recent weeks Justice had become something like a father to Eli. The boy practically idolized Justice, who was kind without doting on the boy. How many times had she discovered Justice teaching Eli how to do something? Too many to count.

And the man was a good teacher, clear and concise and patient with her son.

It was apparent to anyone with eyes that Justice adored the boy and wanted him to grow up to be a good man.

For her part, Nora had been so busy just trying to survive over the last couple of years it had never even occurred to her how important it was for Eli to have a man to look up to and learn from. The notion hadn't even entered her mind. Life had thrown them a hard turn, and it had been all that she could do—more than she could do, in fact—to just keep things together.

Thank the Lord that Justice had come along. He had

already fixed so many things. The ranch looked better than ever.

But it wasn't just the state of the place that hummed. It was state of them, the state of Eli and Nora herself, now that this man was among them.

Justice had filled a void she hadn't previously allowed herself to even consider.

Considering it now, Nora blushed again realizing she was in love with the man.

Which was pure foolishness, of course.

Not that there was anything wrong with the idea. She was still a young woman, and life would be better with a man, especially a kind, hardworking man who treated her son well.

Also, she had known Justice longer than she had known Blake when her deceased husband had asked to marry her.

And she hadn't just known Justice longer. She knew him better as well.

You nurse a man back to health then spend another six weeks living and working together, you get to know each other. They talked at mealtimes and lingered in conversation most nights after Eli went to sleep.

He was younger than Blake. Justice didn't remember how old he was, but she figured he was in his late twenties or thirty at the oldest.

And handsome? Once the bruises and swelling had departed, his face set her heart to fluttering.

Watching him swing the ax and split wood with a single strike, her heart fluttered again, this time in reaction to his rippling muscles and the smooth, graceful way he set his body in motion.

Yes, Justice had reawakened the woman in her, she was ashamed to confess.

Again, her attraction was sensible enough in terms of Justice and the time they had spent together.

What made no sense was attaching herself to a man with no past.

For no man truly lacked history.

Justice had a past. He just couldn't remember it.

And what all did that past entail?

Who was he?

What was his real name?

Where was he from?

Why was he so good with Eli, so easy with her?

Though it pained her to admit it, he lacked the awkwardness and coarseness she'd witnessed in most bachelors.

He rode easily in the saddle of family life as only a family man could.

Somewhere, he likely had a wife and children.

Her heart ached at the thought of losing him. Which again was absurd. But the human heart doesn't give a hoot about logic, and the absurdity of her situation didn't change how she felt.

Nora had never been a particularly emotional woman. Or rather, she had never allowed herself to show her full emotions. And she had guarded them even more closely since Blake had passed because his death had left her alone with a failing ranch to run and a young son to raise.

But with Justice she'd let her guard down. With his many positive qualities, easy smiles, and the natural way he fit among them, how couldn't she let her guard down? Sitting around the dinner table, she found herself grinning and laughing and feeling young again.

Yes, that was part of it, too. With Justice around she not only felt like a woman again, she also felt young again.

It felt good.

But she was kidding herself, savoring something sweet that was destined to turn sour.

For one day, she knew, he would leave them. Either to search out his past or because he remembered the people he had left behind.

And then, oh Nora, you will be more alone than you've ever been before.

Without intending to she took a step toward the open door, toward Justice. But she froze in the doorway staring out at the happy scene: Eli handing Justice another log; Justice nodding at him and saying something she couldn't hear, something that made the boy smile; the dog lying a short distance away, panting happily and watching the man he loved, the man they all had come to love.

Again, she blushed and felt her heart flutter.

Love?

What had gotten into her?

Nothing. Nothing had gotten into her. Nothing but the truth, that was.

She did love him.

She suspected he had feelings for her, too. A woman could tell. The way he looked at her, the things he said, the way he'd brought her that flower the previous morning saying how it matched her eyes.

Justice was too much of a gentleman to say anything more direct, but sometimes she wished he would.

Suddenly, she felt a wild desire to run outside and tell Justice how much she loved him and to ask him to stay forever.

But she could never do that, no matter how much she wanted him to stay.

Because the ghost of his mysterious past haunted her day and night.

Did it haunt him, too?

Likely. He never said as much, but she wondered if he was just staying here to pay off an imagined debt.

She knew he wanted to track down his killers and avenge himself upon them. She had prayed for nothing less, had prayed not only for his life but also for vengeance.

But now, the thought terrified her.

For how could one man possibly face four hardened killers and hope to survive?

CHAPTER 7

"Watch out now, Eli," Justice said, ready to shoe the mare's final hoof.

"It's okay, sir. Daisy don't kick."

"All guns are loaded, son, and all horses kick. You keep those things in mind, you'll save a lot of trouble. And all dogs bite."

"Not Rafer."

"No, not Rafer. He won't bite us, anyway. But he did a pretty good job on that rattler this morning."

The boy laughed.

Then, as if taking issue with their conversation, the big mutt huffed twice and started growling.

Justice turned and saw a lone rider approaching.

Obviously not Diego, given the dog's reaction. Rafer trotted out of the stable, head low, tail high, fur raised up between his shoulders.

Justice patted Eli on the back. "Get on inside, boy. Tell your mama we got a visitor."

"Yes sir."

"But Eli? Tell her to stay inside till I see what's what."

"Yes sir," Eli said and sprinted off faster than a scalded cat.

The rider drew closer.

Justice's hand went reflexively to his hip but found only the cloth of the britches that were too short for him. He might not remember his past, but his body had memories of its own. In this case memories of handling a firearm.

But he had no pistol. So holding only the farrier hammer, he pulled down the brim of the hat and walked out to meet the stranger.

At least I've got the sun to my back.

The thought came out of nowhere, and he might've questioned its origin if the man, drawing close now, hadn't spoken.

"Who are you?" the man said, sounding annoyed. He was young, maybe twenty or twenty-one, and brown-haired. He wore filthy duds, a gun belt, and a frown.

Stepping closer Justice experienced a twinge of unease—not fear but caution—triggered less by the man's gun or expression and more by the face itself.

The rider looked familiar... and not in a good way.

"You got it all wrong, stranger," Justice said. "I didn't ride onto your ranch. You rode in here. What's your name?"

"Where's the woman at?"

"I asked you your name."

"And I asked you yours. Now, tell me where the woman's at. I heard she's a looker and came to see for myself."

"You ride for Tucker?"

"Yeah, not that it's any business of yours. Fetch the woman."

"She doesn't want to talk to you. She's not selling. No matter what he offers."

"Shoot," the man laughed. "Tucker didn't send me. I'm not here for him. Or you. I'm here for the widow." He laid a hand

33

on the butt of his pistol. "You got three seconds to fetch that woman."

"Or what? You'll shoot an unarmed man?"

The rider chuckled. "Won't be the first time. Or the last."

The ranch house door banged open, and Nora filled its frame lifting the rifle to her shoulder. "It's Tate!"

The rider yanked the pistol from its holster.

Justice whipped his arm and hurled the hammer, which struck Tate in the face just as the outlaw was lifting his revolver.

Tate's head jerked sharply backward and the gun discharged into the dirt.

The horse reared, and Tate fell limply off its back and hit the hard ground.

A second later Rafer was on him. The big mutt's jaws closed on Tate's throat. Rafer shook his head back and forth, growling fiercely through a mouthful of man flesh.

"Drop it," Justice said, and the dog stepped back panting and bright-eyed, his jaws foamed with blood.

Justice patted the dog's head and, crouching down, saw that Rafer's attack had been unnecessary.

He had made a lucky throw with that hammer. Lucky enough that even lightning couldn't bring Tate back to life, not with a hole like that in his forehead.

Nora and Eli came running out, but Justice raised a hand. He didn't want them seeing the mess.

"Y'all go back inside the house," he said in a calm voice. "I'll take care of this."

"Are you hurt?" Nora asked.

"Not a scratch," Justice said.

"Is he dead?" Eli asked in a small voice.

"He's gone, son. You don't have to worry about him. Now, go on, both of you. Get back in the house."

"Okay, Justice," Nora said. He was pleased to see that she was holding it together. "I'm glad you're okay."

"Me too," Justice said, showing her a grin. "I reckon Tate probably has a bounty on him. After I finish shoeing Daisy, I'll take him into town and see."

As Nora and Eli went inside, Justice glanced over at Tate's horse. The bay had retreated only a short distance. It stood at the trough drinking.

Which meant two things: it was thirsty and no stranger to violence.

Justice picked up Tate's pistol, an 1851 Colt Navy that looked like it hadn't been cleaned in a long time.

He shook his head feeling deep disdain for any man who neglected his woman, his animals, or his firearms.

At least the pistol had been converted. He unfastened Tate's gun belt and counted the cartridges.

Thirteen.

He flipped open the gate, meaning to add a round, but left one chamber empty to avoid accidental discharge, and returned the revolver to its holster, which he fastened around his hips.

He'd clean the Colt before heading to town.

Meanwhile, he searched Tate and his saddlebags finding another 20 shells for the pistol, a wallet with a surprising 72 dollars inside, a pouch of tobacco, some pigging strips, and a bone-handled knife.

Was this the knife the blond-haired one used to cut off my shirt?

And what had Tate been planning to do with Nora?

Didn't matter now.

Tate was dead. That's what mattered.

One down, three to go.

CHAPTER 8

Justice reckoned he knew where he could find the other killers. If Tate rode for Tucker, the other three probably did, too. That meant trouble for Nora and Diego and all these small ranchers, but it also made Justice's job easier because in country like this, half the battle was figuring out where to find your quarry.

These notions occurred to him effortlessly, as if coming out of some deep, disremembered well of hunting bad men.

He gentled Tate's gelding with considerable ease. There was no need to lasso the horse. Justice simply passed it by, then came back past talking softly, letting the bay get used to his presence and his voice.

He gave the gelding some hay. As the horse ate he spoke softly and smoothed one big hand over the beast's neck.

Then he retrieved the tack hammer, cleaned it off, and turned his attention back to Daisy and her final shoe.

He let Tate lie in the dirt. The man had done his best to kill Justice and left him for dead, then had been planning to shoot Nora... among other things.

Justice felt no remorse over what he'd done and no duty to the outlaw's remains.

When he finished with Daisy he went back to the ranch house and held Tate's wallet out to Nora. "There's 72 dollars. I want you to have it."

Nora looked at the wallet but didn't take it. "That's very kind of you, Justice, but you killed the man. By the law of the land that money's yours."

"And I want you to have it. I'll never be able to repay you for saving my life, nursing me back to health, and putting me up these last several weeks, but maybe this money will help a touch."

"There is no debt, Justice. Besides, even if there were you've worked it off."

"Not hardly. Take the money, Nora."

She shook her head. She said nothing for a few seconds, staring not at the wallet but at him, her blue eyes shining brightly with emotion. "If there were a debt I wouldn't want you to pay it off. We enjoy your company, Justice. Very much so, in fact. I'd sooner have you here with us than have ten thousand dollars handed to me."

Justice smiled and wanted very much to haul this brave, beautiful woman into an embrace. And more than that. He wanted to taste her kiss and confess his deep fondness and to hear those words reciprocated by her.

But that wouldn't be fair to Nora. Or to Eli, who stood not ten feet away hanging on every word.

Justice loved this woman and wanted to share his life with her, but how could he when tomorrow he might wake up and remember another woman, another child, another life?

"I'll be sticking around a while, if you'll have me," he said, "so don't take the notion that I'm paying my final tab."

Nora's shoulders relaxed and she allowed a small smile.

"I'm glad to hear that, Justice. Very glad. I'm certain Eli is, too."

He thrust the wallet toward her again. "Now, take the money."

Nora shook her head. "If you insist on sharing the money with me, please take it to town with you and put a portion against my tab at Mueller's Mercantile. But perhaps you should hold back a few dollars and find a shirt and britches that actually fit you."

With this comment Nora smiled playfully, and Justice was seized with an almost irresistible urge to haul her into his arms and kiss her.

He did resist the urge, however. Barely.

Behind Nora, Eli asked, "You promise you're coming back, Justice?"

"Count on it, son."

The boy smiled brightly.

"In the meantime, I want you to keep an eye on things around here, okay?"

Eli nodded and squared his shoulders.

"Look," Justice told Nora, "I don't think anybody's going to bother you while I'm away. How far is Dos Pesos?"

"Five miles give or take."

He nodded. "So an hour unless this bay gives me trouble."

"You can take Daisy."

"And mess up those new shoes? Pshaw. Eli and I worked too hard on those. Isn't that right, son?"

Grinning, Eli nodded.

Justice mussed the boy's straw-colored hair then told Nora, "Thank you but I want to try the bay. For as worthless as Tate was, I suspect he owned a good horse. I'll give the gelding a bit longer to rest then see how he rides. While I'm gone, stick inside. Keep the rifle and the Colt ready. Rafer'll let you know if anyone comes. Again, I don't expect trouble, but better safe than sorry."

"All right," Nora said. "But Justice? What if those other three men are in Dos Pesos? What if they see you?"

He smiled. "Well, I reckon that would save me a good deal of hunting, anyway. Wherever they are, I suppose we know something about them now."

"They ride for Tucker?"

"Seems likely. Men like these range in packs."

Nora nodded grimly. "So they'll come looking for him."

"Perhaps. But I kindly doubt it. Tate said he wasn't here on Tucker's business. He said he'd heard you were pretty and wanted to see for himself. I believe he was sniffing around of his own accord."

Nora looked disgusted. "I hate to think what he would have done if—"

Justice touched her arm gently. "No need to let your mind wander. That man's dead as dead can be. He can't hurt anybody ever again."

He went outside and tied the stiffening corpse to the back of the bay. Justice was glad Tate wasn't a heavy man. He was even gladder that the bay didn't protest.

"You might even be a better horse than I'm hoping," Justice said, caressing the white star that blazed on the gelding's nose.

The thought pleased Justice, because if he was riding toward the things he expected, he'd be needing a good horse that didn't mind blood or gunfire.

CHAPTER 9

If the hour-long ride to Dos Pesos was any indication, the bay truly was even better than Justice had hoped. The horse reacted to his every command, no matter how subtle.

The whole ride Justice spoke softly to the animal, wanting it to know his voice. When he got the gelding home, he would continue to speak to it as he rubbed it down and fed it a bait of oats and prepared a stall.

Entering town, he drew many stares. Or rather, Tate drew them. People stopped on the boards and pointed at the body tied behind Justice.

Boys appeared from here and there, scampering seemingly out of thin air in the manner of boys everywhere, and followed him as he rode down the dusty main street surveying the storefronts.

He passed a livery, two saloons, the Dos Pesos Bank, and a bordello before spotting one of the buildings he was hunting for.

Mueller's Mercantile was a big place and looked well-kept from the outside.

He did not stop. Not yet.

Instead, he rode on down the street until he came to the sheriff's office. By now, a pack of a dozen boys trailed him. He ignored them and went inside.

The sheriff sat behind his desk eating a bowl of dark brown stew. He wore a bib over his shirt but dark stains streaked his graying beard.

"What can I do for you?" the sheriff asked, pushing his meal aside.

Justice introduced himself.

"Justice?" the sheriff asked. "You got a first name?"

"Mister'll do."

"Mister Justice, huh?" the sheriff said amiably. "With a name like that I have to ask if you're looking to hire on as a deputy."

"Not today, thanks," Justice said, then explained why he was there.

The sheriff, who introduced himself as Pat Perkins, nodded taking it all in. "Tate, you say? I might know the name. Let me have a look at him."

They went outside. Perkins shooed the boys who were gathered around the dead man like so many ghouls.

Perkins grabbed Tate unceremoniously by the hair and lifted his face. "I've seen him around once or twice. Came into town with Tucker's crew. Stirred up some trouble just last weekend. No shooting, but they knocked the teeth out of Garrett Fontaine and left him laying there."

Perkins let Tate's head drop, then spat in the dust. "Good riddance. Let's see if there's any paper on him."

There was.

Aloysius Tate was wanted in Texas for rape, cattle rustling, and pistol-whipping a rancher to death.

They unloaded the body and suddenly, Justice was two hundred dollars richer.

"Might want to spend some of that on a good rifle,"

Perkins said. "Tucker's crew is a big outfit. Rowdy, too. Act like they own the place. I don't reckon they'll take too kindly to you gunning down one of their own."

"Truth be told, I didn't gun him down. I killed him with a tack hammer."

A grin split the sheriff's beard. "A tack hammer, huh? Resourceful. That'll serve you well in this country. But I'm serious about Tucker's crew. Watch your back, all right?"

"Will do, sheriff. Thanks, and good to meet you."

Justice led the bay back down the street, speaking softly to him every step. He tethered the horse outside Mueller's Mercantile and went inside, followed at a distance by several fascinated boys.

Inside, he introduced himself to Mr. Mueller, a dapper, middle-aged man in a black waistcoat and gold-rimmed spectacles.

The merchant smiled warmly and smiled even more warmly when Justice explained he was staying at the Eckert place and had come to settle Nora's tab, which totaled 47 dollars.

Justice handed Mueller 50 of Tate's dollars. "Keep the change. I reckon you took a risk keeping Nora and Eli from starving out there."

Mueller nodded. "I have a soft spot for widows and children."

"That makes two of us, Mr. Mueller," Justice said and pointed to the rack of rifles behind the counter. "Is that a 73?"

"Yes sir. A Winchester 1873 in .44-40. Brand new and yours for only 25 dollars. Just got two in. And if you're in the market for a pistol, I just so happen to have an 1873 Colt Single Action Model P also chambered in .44-40. Your cartridges would be compatible with the Winchester."

Justice asked to see the rifle and pistol alike. Both felt so natural in his hands he was virtually certain he'd carried them in the past.

He turned the pistol and read the words etched into the barrel: *Colt Frontier Six-Shooter*.

"I'll take the six-shooter and both rifles," he said, "and 300 rounds of ammunition."

He traded in Tate's misused Colt Navy and gun belt for a black, flat-crowned hat and a new gun belt that fit him more comfortably.

Next, he bought a breech-loading, double-barrel shotgun and a big box of shells. The rifles would go a long way in defending the ranch, but if a bunch of Tate's friends showed up and some of them made it to the house, that shotgun would prove the wisest purchase he had ever made. Anybody, even a young boy, could hit a man at close range with a scattergun.

Between those weapons and the presence of Rafer, Justice would feel better about leaving the ranch to track down his other three murderers.

Finally, he purchased 100 rounds for the Sharps, making a mental note to return the ammunition Diego had lent him. Then, satisfied with his firearm purchases, he walked the store with Mueller and bought a pair of field glasses, a good deal of flour and sugar, a pound of tea, and two pounds of Arbuckles.

His body practically pounced on the coffee, which he hadn't tasted during this second life. His strong craving was another clue to the man he'd been before, he supposed.

He picked up a few pieces of hard candy, a slate, and chalk for Eli, along with everything he needed to strengthen and expand Nora's stable and to build her a small smokehouse.

He stopped at the end of the aisle and stared for a

moment at the pretty blue-and-white gingham dress displayed there. "I reckon I best get one of those, too."

Mr. Mueller nodded, jotting it down, and said he had Mrs. Eckert's measurements somewhere if the dress was for her.

"It is. Now, I'd best see about getting some clothes that fit me, too. I'll be needing two pairs."

While Mr. Mueller set to preparing his order, Justice strapped on his new gun belt. His hands adjusted everything, his body telling him exactly how he liked to wear the thing. Its fit and the weight of the new Colt felt good now, natural, like a thing he'd been missing without knowing.

He crossed the street to the barber shop where he met the barber, Alfredo Barrera, and ordered a hot bath, a shave, and a haircut.

When Justice disrobed, Barrera stared with disbelief at the many scars. He had obviously been shot, stabbed, burned, and even whipped in the past. Then Justice turned around, and the barber's eyes locked onto the silver badge half-melted into his chest.

"Don't ask," Justice said, sinking into the warm water. "It's a long story I'd rather not tell."

Barrera gave a slight bow. "I take very seriously the preferences of men with many scars." He went about his business with no further questions.

It felt good to be clean again. Looking in the mirror Justice felt a flicker of recognition he hadn't experienced when observing his dirty, bearded countenance.

He still remembered nothing solid, but there was a sense of familiarity there, a sense of something being as it should.

He thanked Barrera, tipped him generously, and headed back to the mercantile, stopping to speak softly once more to the bay before going back inside.

Justice still had 49 dollars in his wallet.

The 200 dollars he'd earned for bagging Tate was more than a laborer might expect for six months of hard work.

Considering that and the money he'd gotten from Tate's wallet, he reckoned there was good money in killing bad men.

Which suited him just fine, since he had three more to track down.

CHAPTER 10

Riding back onto the ranch Justice was happy to see no new tracks along the trail.

As Justice came into view of the house, Rafer gave a single bark, hailing the house. A moment later the slender dark line of the Sharps barrel slid through the window.

But then the dog recognized him and trotted forward, tail wagging. The barrel slid back into the house, the door opened, and Nora and Eli came out smiling in the sunlight.

It felt good returning, especially because he was carting supplies and had a good deal of cash remaining. The other supplies would arrive soon, Justice having hired the freight.

The dog, who must've been confused by Justice's change in appearance and smell, circled the bay once, tail knocking happily back and forth, then trotted alongside them as they ambled over to the ranch house.

"I didn't even recognize you, Justice!" Eli exclaimed. "I sure do like that hat!"

Justice touched its brim and smiled down at the boy. "Well then, next time I'm in town, I'll have to see about getting one in your size."

Nora smiled up at him, her blue eyes glittering. "You certainly clean up nice, Mr. Justice." She touched her own hair absentmindedly. "Though now I feel utterly self-conscious."

Justice dismounted. "Hogwash. You are a beautiful woman, Nora, an incredibly beautiful woman."

Nora's smile widened, but then she chuckled lightly, looking at the ground, and surprised Justice by blushing.

"Don't tease me, please," she said in a quiet voice.

"Tease you?" he said. "I speak only the truth." Then, not wanting to make her uncomfortable, he changed the subject telling her he'd paid off her tab at Mueller's.

Explaining the money he had gotten for turning in Tate, he handed Nora 25 dollars. "That's half of what's left. Tomorrow, you can ride into town and get whatever else you want. I got your flour and sugar and a few other things. Most of it'll be riding with the building materials that should be here later this afternoon. Next time, I reckon we should take your wagon to town and save on freighting costs. But anyway, I just got what I could think of. I'm sure there are all sorts of things there you might need or want."

A beaming Nora held the money against her bosom. "Why thank you, Justice. Thank you so much."

Then, impulsively, she hugged him.

Justice stiffened with surprise but quickly recovered, wrapped his arms around her, and held her for several seconds.

It was their first time touching like this.

Nora felt good in his arms, wonderful in fact, and when they finally broke their embrace and she stepped back smoothing her dress and blushing again, he sorely missed the feel of her.

Eli grinned looking between them. Six or not he had seen

something pass between the adults. He clearly liked what he had seen and wanted to see more of it.

Nothing would please Justice more. But of course, that was not possible. Not until he solved the mystery of his missing past.

"Don't know if you have one of these already," he said, unpacking the slate, "but I hadn't seen one around, so I thought maybe—"

"How very kind of you," Nora said, and she turned to Eli with a wide smile. "This is for learning to write and add. And look, Eli, its edges are even wrapped in leather. What a wonderful gift."

"Thank you, Justice!"

"You're welcome, partner. And here. It'll work better with this." He pulled the chalk from his shirt pocket and handed it over.

"Thank you!" Eli said, clearly overjoyed with his present.

"If you work hard and apply yourself, I'll get you a McGuffey reader, too."

Eli nodded like a man starting a new job and determined to make a name for himself. "Yes sir. I will work hard."

Smiling, Justice tousled the boy's blond hair. Then he reached into his pocket. "I almost forgot. There's one more thing. You know anybody who likes candy?"

"Yeah," the boy shouted. "Me!"

"Well then, I guess I better give these to you."

Eli thanked him as he took the candy and stared at it with great reverence.

"That was very kind of you, Justice. You may eat one piece today, Eli. This is a special treat. I won't have you gobbling it all up."

"Yes ma'am."

Justice opened the saddle bags.

"Coffee and tea?" Nora said, looking almost as excited as Eli with his candy. "My but that sounds like heaven."

"I agree. What do you say we celebrate and put on some Arbuckles right now?"

"That sounds wonderful, Justice."

He pulled one of the Winchesters from its scabbard. "While it's brewing I'll show you two how to use one of these. I bought a pair of them, along with a double-barrel shotgun."

Nora took the lever-action rifle and examined it gravely. "You think they'll come looking for Tate?"

"I don't know, but I reckon we'd best assume they will come for one thing or another. That way we won't be caught unawares. But that doesn't mean we should stop living life or enjoying it. In fact, only by preparing for violence can we truly relax and enjoy life. So here, Nora. I got you something else. Hope you don't mind me taking the liberty."

Opening the other pack he pulled out the dress, which Mueller had boxed up for him.

"For me?" Nora said, accepting the box. When she lifted the lid her mouth dropped open. She pulled the dress free and held it up, letting it unfurl like a blue-and-white gingham flag.

"Oh, Justice," Nora said.

She looked from the dress to him, her blue eyes glistening. Her mouth wriggled, and he understood she was on the verge of tears.

"I'm sorry, Nora. If you don't like it—"

"I love it," she said. "I have never seen such a beautiful dress. Thank you so much."

Then she was in his arms again hugging him hard.

Loving the feel of her body against his, Justice was suddenly more motivated than ever to hunt down those other three men. The sooner he did, the sooner he could start tracking down his past and see if making a life with Nora was in the cards.

He sure hoped it was.

CHAPTER 11

The next day Nora emerged from the ranch house wearing her new blue-and-white gingham dress. Having bathed and pulled her long, blond hair back into a thick braid, she looked absolutely stunning from head to toe.

Eli gaped at her. "You look real pretty, Ma."

"From the mouths of babes," Justice said. "You are a sight to behold, ma'am."

Nora smiled brightly then blushed and averted her eyes, clearly both pleased and embarrassed by their praise.

Justice laid down his tools and hitched the mules and readied the wagon, which the three of them took to Dos Pesos riding together like a happy family.

"It feels so good to be riding into town without the shame and worry of the mercantile debt. Thank you again, Justice."

"It was my deepest pleasure to help especially after all that you've done for me these last many weeks."

In Dos Pesos Nora's beauty drew many stares. Justice felt proud to be seen with her.

For her own part Nora seemed unaware of the attention as she went about her business, purchasing a few more supplies from Mueller's before Justice treated her and Eli to lunch at the Dos Pesos Inn.

The enchiladas and tamales were delicious, and the cold beer was the best thing Justice ever remembered tasting.

Though even the beer paled in comparison with his enjoyment of watching a very happy Nora tuck a stray lock of golden hair behind her ear or watching her overjoyed son flash a smile while savoring his sarsaparilla.

"It is so nice to be enjoying a meal I didn't cook myself," Nora said.

Justice smiled across the table at her. "Well, in that case, we'll have to come back again sometime."

He paid for the meal and gave the waitress, a pleasant young woman named Juanita, a full dime as a tip.

"*Muchas gracias, señor.*"

"*De nada.*"

Though he had no recollection of how he had come to speak Spanish, Justice knew the language as well as he knew English—a fortuitous discovery, considering most folks in these parts spoke Spanish.

He held the door for Nora and Eli and had to resist the natural temptation to take Nora's arm out on the street.

Eli scrambled into the wagon quick as a squirrel. Nora smiled sweetly as Justice helped her up.

"Thank you so much for a wonderful outing, Justice. I will never forget it."

"Nor will I," Justice said. He climbed up and started toward home.

The next few days were pleasant. He rose and began working early each morning, pleased to be joined almost immediately by Eli. Justice explained everything he was doing as he saw to various repairs and built the new smokehouse.

The boy happily gobbled up all this information and did his best to help.

Rafer stuck close, drowsing but never really sleeping, a half-wild beast Justice had come to appreciate.

Apparently, Justice had done a fair amount of building in his past because the planning and seeing through of this work was as effortless to him as speaking Spanish or handling livestock.

Which, of course, made him wonder again who he had been in his prior life, where he was from, and what he had done.

For all his curiosity, however, he dreaded the day he would finally uncover that missing life, because he had grown to love this one so much and could imagine no existence on Earth to match the joy of life with Nora and Eli.

And yet a man cannot simply do what he wishes. He must honor his commitments. Even those obscured by amnesia.

Eventually, he would need to track down the truth of his past.

What if he did have a wife and children?

Could he ever love them again having known Nora and Eli?

Yes.

He would have to even if his heart couldn't fathom such a thing now, full as it was with love for Nora and Eli.

If he had already promised himself to others, he would honor that promise no matter how painful. After all, what was love if not protecting and providing for those who needed you?

No matter what happened he would continue to care for Nora and Eli and to help them however he could, but the questions of his past reined in his current desires, so he minded his manners and continued to sleep in the barn.

One night, doing just that, he awoke to the sound of distant gunfire.

A far-off pop, then another, then a rapid string of faint gunshots, what sounded like several people firing at the same time.

Then it was over.

He sat up gripping the Winchester and listening, Rafer alert beside him.

Where had it been?

It sounded like it had come from the southwest, but he knew that in country like this, distance and topography could twist sounds like a branching, meandering stream redirects water.

In the morning over *huevos rancheros* and coffee, he reminded Nora to keep the firearms close and explained he was going to pay Diego a visit.

Following her directions he rode the bay to the neighboring ranch, where a cowhand with a scattergun stopped him at the gate.

The man escorted him past a small bunkhouse to Diego's home, a small yet well-kept ranch house surrounded by flowers and foraging chickens.

Diego came out and greeted him.

They shook hands and Diego introduced his wife, Eugenia, who was a tiny, white-haired woman with a pretty smile and the breezy warmth of a Southern lady.

Once Eugenia had gone back inside, Justice handed Diego a parcel. "I owed you this. Thanks again. We might've needed those."

Opening the parcel Diego raised a snowy eyebrow. "This is more cartridges than I gave you."

"Consider it interest on a much-needed loan," Justice said, and handed him a second package.

Diego smiled at the tobacco pouch. "Well, now I'm really

hoping you come to your senses and make a life with Nora and Eli. You appear to be a neighbor of the highest order. So, what'd you do, strike silver over there? You clearly came into some money."

Justice explained what happened with Tate.

"Two hundred dollars, huh? That'll buy a whole lot a tack hammers. Tucker ain't fired back yet?"

Justice shook his head. "I don't think he knows even. Tate was riding solo looking for Nora. He said as much. And considering the charges against him back in Texas, I think his intentions were less than honorable."

Diego spat on the hard-packed earth. "Wish you'd only winged him. There's a man who deserved to be staked out Apache-style."

Justice told the old rancher about the gunshots he'd heard in the night.

Diego nodded. He had six ranch hands. Of late, they'd been keeping a watch at night.

This morning they had reported gunshots to the south.

"I was just getting ready to check on the Lopez place if you care to come along," Diego said.

"Let's ride."

CHAPTER 12

An eerie stillness reigned as Justice and Diego approached the Lopez house.

Diego looked around warily. "Awful quiet around here."

"I was just thinking the same thing." Justice widened the gap between his horse and Diego's. If something went wrong here, they'd be better off with some space between them.

Diego pulled his rifle from its boot. "The Lopezes have a dog, but he ain't barking."

As they drew closer to the house, Justice nodded to a dark shape lying between the house and the stable. "There's the dog." Then, trotting ahead, he raised his voice. "Hello, the house!"

A rifle barked from inside the house, and halfway to Justice the bullet kicked up dust.

The bay stepped back but didn't panic.

"Next shot, I'll knock you out of your saddle," a woman's voice cried, high with terror. "Get out of here. There will be no other warning."

"We mean no harm," Justice said, holding his hands up so she could see they were empty.

"Mrs. Lopez, this is Diego Contreras," Diego said in Spanish. "The man with me is a friend. He's been staying with Nora Eckert next door. We heard gunshots in the night and wanted to check on you folks."

The door opened and they were welcomed inside by an apologetic Antonia Lopez, who thanked them for coming.

As soon as Justice stepped inside he smelled the iron tang of blood. Roberto Lopez lay atop a pallet in the kitchen attended by his two teenage daughters, whose eyes were red and puffy.

Roberto sat up with a grimace. A bloody bandage was wrapped around his left arm and a minor laceration glistened across one cheek, red and gray beneath the grease.

"Looks like you got lucky," Justice said. "Grazed your cheek. An inch to one side, we wouldn't be talking."

"I don't feel so lucky," Roberto said, looking very pale and clearly in a lot of pain. He pulled back the blanket to show the blood-soaked bandages covering the worst of his injuries, where he'd taken a bullet to the hip.

"You're gonna need a doctor," Justice said. "Think you can make the trip to town?"

Roberto spread his hands indicating the makeshift kitchen bed. "I couldn't even make it into the bedroom. But with your help and a little mescal, yes."

Justice turned to Diego. "Is there a doctor in Dos Pesos?"

"Alfredo Barrera, the barber, doubles as a surgeon. He'll help. And he's an honest man. If Roberto's injuries require a more experienced surgeon, he'll tell us. That happens, we'll go to Santa Fe."

Justice turned back to the Lopezes. "Tell me about the rustlers."

"They weren't rustlers," Roberto said, wincing at a sudden pain. "Yes, they took some of our stock, but that wasn't why they came."

"Diablos," Antonia Lopez said.

Roberto nodded, and the girls began to cry. "First, they shot the dog. Then they started yelling at us, demanding we leave, promising to do horrible things if we didn't leave our ranch."

Antonia shuddered. "They threatened to kill Roberto and use my daughters and me."

"I went outside and demanded they leave," Roberto said.

"And they gunned him down," Antonia said. "So I shot at them from the window. I hit one of them, maybe two, and they rode off."

"Good work," Justice said.

"Yes, but even if I had killed all of them, it would not restore Roberto's health. Everything is lost. This ranch was our dream, our home, but now—" She broke down crying.

"We must not surrender," Roberto said. "This is still our dream, still our home."

Justice asked, "How many riders were there?"

"Four."

"Were they wearing masks?"

"No."

"You recognize any of them?"

Roberto shook his head. "It was dark. The only one I really saw was the one who did most of the talking."

"What did he look like?"

"He was big, built like a bull."

"Red hair?"

Lopez nodded. "You know him?"

"Not really. But I'm going to. His name's Del Mundo."

"He one of them boys you're hunting?" Diego asked.

Justice nodded but said nothing more. None of this surprised him, least of all Del Mundo's involvement, but he had learned one piece of valuable information.

Del Mundo and his riders feared death. Not all men did.

But when Mrs. Lopez had opened fire they had fled. Harder outlaws would have spread out and finished the job.

So yes, Del Mundo feared death. That was a thing to remember, a thing that might help Justice anticipate Del Mundo's actions and reactions down the line.

"I'm sorry this happened to you folks," Justice said. "I can't change that, but we'll do what we can for you."

Diego nodded. "Let's get Roberto to the doctor. Mrs. Lopez, you and your daughters are welcome to stay at my ranch until things get back to normal. We'd be happy to have you."

"Thank you, Señor Contreras, but I have a sister in Dos Pesos. We will stay with her. I would feel safer in town, and I want to be close to Roberto as he recovers."

With the help of her daughters, Mrs. Lopez gathered the essentials while Justice and Diego readied the wagon. Thankfully, the rustlers had not stolen the mules.

"You mind escorting them to town and getting him to the doctor?" Justice asked.

"I can do that," Diego said, and narrowed his eyes. "You ain't fixing to do something dumb, are you?"

Justice pointed to the rustler's tracks. "I'm going to follow these tracks and see where they take me."

"I think I can guess where they'll take you."

Justice nodded. "Yeah, same here, but I aim to take the guessing out of it."

"Tucker's men are rough. They're just as likely to shoot as speak."

"I'm not looking to speak. Or shoot. Not yet, anyway. I just want to follow these tracks. Then, I'll report my findings to Sheriff Perkins."

Diego shook his head. "That won't do no good."

"Is Perkins in Tucker's pocket?"

"Nah, I doubt it. Perkins is a good enough old boy, but

he's no pistolero. This whole territory is full of outgunned lawmen without the sand to make a stand. And Perkins is right at home with them."

Justice nodded, taking it all in, unsurprised but not wholly convinced. He'd need to prod Perkins a little and see where he really stood. "All right then. I'm still going to track these men and report what I find. Then, if someone forces my hand, I'll feel better about what follows, knowing I tried to do things legally."

"Well, if it comes to shooting, you won't be alone," Diego said. "I might be old, but I still have some fight left in me, and a couple of my cow punchers know how to handle themselves." He spat again. "Tucker should know better than to mess with men like us."

"What do you mean, men like us?"

Diego grinned, one side of his white mustache lifting against his dark face. "I'm so old I have nothing to lose, and you're so mean even dying didn't stop you."

CHAPTER 13

J ustice helped load Roberto into the wagon, then rode south following the tracks. He rode slowly scanning the country ahead, watching for movement or plumes of dust or the flash of metal or glass in the distance.

The rustlers might have left a man with a Sharps along their back trail.

But Justice doubted it. These men didn't expect anyone to follow. They weren't cautious; they were audacious. They had attacked brazenly by night, not even bothering with masks, then stuck together during their retreat keeping the stolen cattle in a single herd, not even attempting to mislead potential pursuers.

Unsurprisingly, their tracks led straight to Tucker's northern gate.

Justice reined in atop a bluff overlooking the final draw, the gate, and the sprawling valley beyond. The tracks chewed up the ground right to the gate 200 yards away where now stood the only man Justice could see.

So far, the guard didn't seem to notice him.

Justice raised his field glasses and scoped the scene. The

man leaned against the gate looking lost in thought with a rifle slung over one shoulder.

Justice swept the binoculars back and forth glassing the country, and saw no other sign of Tucker's crew.

He lowered the glasses, laid his rifle across his lap, and sat there for the better part of a minute waiting for the guard to notice him, curious as to how the man would react and what he would say.

When at last the man finally noticed Justice, he said nothing at all. He gave a little jump, lifted his rifle, and fired wildly.

A bullet kicked up dirt twenty feet to one side of Justice.

The man worked the lever and corrected his aim.

Before the man could shoot again, however, Justice returned fire. The Winchester bucked against his shoulder, and the man at the gate flew backward, shot in the chest.

Justice sat for a moment, pleased that the bay remained calm beneath him. He considered riding down and collecting the dead man's rifle, wallet, and six-shooter, but the sound of their brief skirmish had no doubt echoed across Tucker's land. The cattle baron's crew might already be riding in this direction.

Justice turned and rode back.

Despite leaving the dead man's possessions behind, this exchange hadn't been a total loss.

The rustlers' bloody infiltration of the Lopez property had been less about the stolen cattle and more about intimidation. Tucker had used it to send a message.

Now, Justice had sent a message of his own.

If Tucker pushed the small ranchers, they would push back.

Hard.

———

WHEN JUSTICE CAME THROUGH THE DOOR, SHERIFF PERKINS had just poured a cup of coffee. His bib lay neatly folded on his desk, and a savory smell hung in the air.

"Mr. Justice," Perkins said pleasantly enough. "What can I do for you today?"

"Gather your deputies, sheriff," Justice said. "You'll need their help making some arrests."

"Slow 'er down, Mr. Justice. Who is it, exactly, you're proposing we take into custody?" Perkins raised his steaming coffee to his bearded lips.

"Sullivan Tucker."

Perkins spat hot coffee across the desk. "What?"

"He's a cattle thief, and his men are guilty of attempted murder." He explained everything that had happened to the Lopezes and the incident at the edge of the properties.

Perkins looked at him like he was crazy. "Let me get this straight. One of Tucker's men shot at you, and you killed him and left him lying there?"

Justice nodded. "I didn't trespass or provoke him in any way. As soon as he saw me, he started shooting. It's a clear case of self-defense."

"So it would seem. Any witnesses?"

"No, but we can ride down there, and you'll see my tracks stop well back from the property line."

Perkins shook his head. "You're out of your mind if you think I'm riding over there with you and arresting Tucker."

"You mean you don't need my help?" Justice said. He had anticipated every turn of this conversation but still wanted to hear it from Perkins. "You and your boys going to arrest him without my assistance?"

Perkins shook his head. "Sullivan Tucker is very power-ful. Probably the wealthiest man in the whole county. And though he might be new to the territory, you sure wouldn't know that by his connections."

"So the law doesn't apply to him?"

"That's not what I'm saying."

"Sure sounds like it to me."

"Look, I'm the law around here, not you."

"Well, then start acting like it. Those men shot Roberto Lopez to pieces and threatened to rape his wife and daughters. If you don't stop them, what good are you?"

Sheriff Perkins set his coffee mug on the desk, hitched his gun belt, and gave Justice his meanest look.

Justice stared back at him with no expression on his face.

The men locked gazes for several silent seconds.

Then Perkins buckled, shaking his head and taking up his coffee mug again. "I do not need this. You have no idea how this county works. My job is dealing with drunks not cattle barons. If I give Tucker trouble, I'll be buzzard bait."

"If you're afraid, Perkins, stay out of it."

"I didn't say—"

"But listen up. If this is your decision, if you're going to stay out of it, stay all the way out, you hear me? Don't give me any trouble."

Perkins sputtered, saying nothing of consequence.

Justice, understanding this as a cowardly man's acquiescence, went out the door.

He crossed the street and went to the barber, ignoring the *closed* sign and going inside where Alfredo Barrera had just finished patching up Roberto Lopez, who was drowsing now beneath a blanket of laudanum and bandages.

Roberto would survive, Barrera explained, but his recovery would take a long time, and it was yet to be seen how well his leg would function, the bullet having nicked the edge of his hip bone.

Whatever the case, the Lopez ranch was in jeopardy.

"You know any men I could hire to help out over there?" Justice said.

"Cowhands?"

"More or less. Men who can work but more importantly, men I can count on in a fight."

Barrera nodded. "I know such men. How many do want to hire?"

"A hundred would be nice, but I reckon I'll start with two. Could you help me with this?"

"No problem at all. Twenty dollars a week."

"For both of them?"

"Yes, that would be for both men. For regular cowboys the price would be less, a dollar a day."

"No, I need men who can handle themselves."

"All right. You are in luck. I know two such men in need of work. I can have them at the Lopez ranch tomorrow morning."

"They're reliable?"

"Yes, very reliable. My cousin, Hector, and his son, Jorge. They returned only recently from the trail and have not yet signed on with another crew."

Justice gave Barrera twenty dollars for the men, added two dollars for the barber's trouble, and crossed the street again to check on the Lopez females, who were staying at the inn until Antonia's sister was ready to take them.

The girls slept on one bed, obviously exhausted by everything they had endured.

Mrs. Lopez stepped into the hall.

Justice decided not to tell her about the incident at the gate. He didn't want to rile her up. But he did tell her about hiring Hector and Jorge Barrera.

"Thank you, Mr. Justice. I will sell some cattle and repay you."

"No need to repay me. Hiring them was my decision, not yours. I do believe, however, you'd be wise to sell off some cattle in order to keep these men on for a while. Otherwise, you might not have any cattle left to sell."

Mrs. Lopez agreed.

"If you like," Justice said, "I'll try to find you a buyer."

"That would be wonderful, Mr. Justice."

"I'll stop by your ranch tomorrow morning, meet these new men, and get them started. I'm sure Mr. Barrera will fill them in, but I want to make sure they understand the situation and the dangers. Then we'll cut out some steers. I should have money for you within the next few days."

With a plan in place, he left the inn and went down the street to where he'd hitched the bay.

As he was untying the horse a deep voice in the street behind him said, "What do you think you're doing with that horse, mister?"

Justice turned and saw a pair of men. One was barely a man, more a grinning young sidekick excited by the confrontation.

The other man, the one who'd spoken, jarred blurry recognition and sharp caution within Justice.

His full beard was as blond as honey, just as Nora had described it.

CHAPTER 14

"What concern is it of yours?" Justice responded. He moved sideways separating himself from the bay knowing what was coming and wanting to protect the gelding.

"That's my friend's horse."

"It's mine now."

"He sell it to you?" The blonde casually raised a hand to his pistol.

Justice did the same. Everything came into crystal clear focus. Every fiber of his body was ready, but his mind grew remarkably calm, slowing the moment, heightening his awareness of everything. "Not exactly. More like he gave it to me. In a manner of speaking."

"You lie. Tate would never part with that gelding let alone give it away."

"He didn't need it anymore."

"Bull. A cowboy needs a horse."

"Not if he's dead."

The blond beard opened as the man gaped at the news.

Now, Justice thought. *Now, while he's rattled.*

That brief advantage would give him all the time he needed to get the drop on the man.

But what then? What would he do if he had his pistol trained on the man's chest?

He couldn't shoot him, not unless he drew too, especially with the crowd now gathering a short distance away. And Justice lacked the authority to arrest these men.

But he didn't want to wait either, didn't want to drag out the moment and give time for the younger man or more friends to get involved or for Sheriff Perkins to come out and blunder things. He wanted to take care of this business now. The key was keeping him rattled while causing him to draw first.

So he stood straighter and pushed his hat back a little. "Don't you recognize me?"

The blonde studied him warily.

Justice stared calmly back at him using his left hand to unbutton his shirt and pull the fabric to one side, exposing the silver star embedded in his chest. "Remember me now?"

The blonde's eyes swelled. "You? It ain't possible. We killed you!" And then, moving jerkily, he hauled his pistol from its holster.

Justice drew smoothly and fired twice, punching one hole through the killer's chest and another through his bushy beard.

The man was dead before he hit the ground.

Two down, two to go.

He turned the smoking barrel on the kid. "Take your hand off that shooting iron, son, or I'll kill you just as dead. That's it. You go ahead and unbuckle that gun belt."

The kid complied.

"That's it. Now step back. Again. All the way back. Get back onto the boardwalk. That's right."

Justice picked up the gun belt, never taking his eyes off

the young man. Only a fool would underestimate a kid. Some of the fastest, deadliest men in the West couldn't grow a full beard yet.

The air was thick with black powder and, oddly, a smell like perfume.

Justice looked around, saw no additional threats, and told the kid, "You can pick up your gun at the sheriff's next time you're in town. Now, where's your buddy's horse?"

"You can't have Josiah's horse."

"Yes, I can. He drew on me, and I killed him. What was his is mine."

"His horse is right over yonder," someone said, "that big strawberry roan in front of the saloon."

"Don't you go trying to steal my horse, too," the kid said.

"Son, I'm no horse thief," Justice said. "I *kill* horse thieves. There's a difference. Now get into the mercantile and don't come out till I'm gone. You come out and I'm still here, I will assume you're coming after me, and you've already seen what happens to men who try me."

The kid did as he was told but paused in the doorway of the mercantile, moving from shocked to surly. "You'll pay for this. We ride for Tucker!"

"Lot of good that did your buddy."

"He has friends. Hard men. They'll be coming for you!"

"Good. I look forward to meeting them again and sorting out our differences."

The kid went inside and closed the door.

Justice took another look around making sure no one was fixing to shoot him in the back. He saw no threats, only the excited citizens of Dos Pesos.

"He killed Josiah Johnson," one boy told another.

"Never seen anyone draw half so fast," a nearby man said in awe.

"Who is he?" a woman asked.

Then Sheriff Perkins came blustering through the crowd holding a scattergun. "What is going on here?"

"He drew on me," Justice said, "but I was faster."

Perkins shook his head. "Why, oh why, did you have to come to my town?"

"Give me a hand carrying him back to your office," Justice said.

Perkins sighed. "Baca, give him a hand, will you? I got a bad back. Besides, this shotgun won't carry itself."

"What's that smell?" Baca asked, giving Justice a hand.

It was Johnson. The man smelled like a perfume factory.

Gagging on the cloying scent, they took the dead man back to the sheriff's office. Holding his nose Baca left quickly.

"Leave that door open," Perkins said. "Johnson smells like a boomtown whore. I don't need him stinking up my office."

Justice ignored the man and closed the door in case anybody came creeping up behind him.

"You got paper on him?" Justice said, unfastening the dead man's gun belt and wrapping it around his own waist. He'd already given Perkins the kid's gun, directing him to hold onto it until he'd cleared out of town.

"Yeah, a hundred and twenty-five dollars, I think."

Justice nodded. That money would allow him to buy some cattle off Mrs. Lopez and expand Nora's stable, which would be necessary, given how many horses he'd been collecting lately. "What was he wanted for?"

"Cattle rustling. Assault. Maybe something else. I think maybe he killed somebody over in the Nations."

"Well, I'll be looking to collect that bounty as soon as you can have it for me."

Perkins paced, ranting about law and order as Justice went through the dead man's pockets. He tossed the tobacco and playing cards aside but took the rest: three double-eagle twenty-dollar gold pieces, a few greenbacks, a big old Bowie knife, and a nice little Remington .41 caliber derringer that he slipped directly into his pocket.

"Speaking of paper," Justice said, turning back to Perkins, "tell me what you have on a couple of men called Del Mundo and Beachem."

CHAPTER 15

Sullivan Tucker paced back and forth in the spacious office of his massive new home. He was a big man with broad shoulders, rough hands, and a large head full of cattle and money. To this point he had bulled his way through life, going from small farmer to cattle baron and, by God, he would bull over any man who attempted to stand in his way now.

"Lopez is still alive?" he asked incredulously.

"So I am told," Haversham said. The tiny, bespectacled lawyer remained in the high-backed chair across from Tucker's desk, a superior grin on his pale face.

Seeing that slick smile Tucker was tempted to pick up the Easterner and snap him over his knee like so much kindling, but Haversham remained valuable. Besides, Haversham was the one man beneath his control whose death would bring consequences down on Tucker.

And Haversham knew it. Hence the smile.

"How is he still alive? Didn't you send four riders? What's it take to hire men who can actually shoot in this country? Back in Texas—"

"With all due respect, sir, you aren't in Texas any longer."

"You think I don't know that? Where is Lopez now?"

"Dos Pesos. From what I understand, he underwent surgery today and is still recuperating in the back room of the barber shop."

"And his family?"

"They've checked into the hotel across the street, sir. Shall I visit them?"

Tucker scratched his big jaw. He needed a shave. He'd see to that as soon as he finished with Haversham. Otherwise, Pearl would point it out.

Sometimes, he wondered why he'd ever bothered to hitch his wagon to a city woman, let alone an Austinite.

Then, in bed, he remembered.

And since coming to the new house where everyone treated him the way he should be treated and where he'd hired folks to cook and clean for his young wife, Pearl had been downright friendly most nights when it was time to hit the hay.

So long as he remembered to shave, he reminded himself.

But first, he had to put this current problem to rest. Pronto. And forever.

Tucker might not come from money like Pearl, and he might not have book learning like the slick and squirrelly Mr. Haversham, but he knew how to fight. And now was the time to finish the Lopezes.

Then, he'd turn his attention to another of the small ranchers. Once he had the valley locked down, he would have proven himself. Then all of this would truly be his. He would be firmly ensconced as the man in New Mexico. Pearl would have nothing to complain about, and he suspected at that point she would be very friendly indeed.

"Yes," he said. "Go pay them a visit. And this time get the

job done, you hear me? Take Del Mundo and Beachem. I want that ranch."

Haversham pushed back his chair and rose, smiling faintly as if Tucker had said something funny, then gave one of his irritating little bows. "It shall be done, sir."

Before he could leave, however, somebody started pounding on the door.

"Come in," Tucker hollered, further irritated by another interruption. What now?

The guard ushered in the new kid and left.

The kid—Tucker couldn't remember his name—stepped forward but stopped halfway to Tucker, holding his hat at his beltline and ringing it like a chicken's neck.

Tucker squinted at the dark stains on the kid's shirt and chaps. Was that blood?

"What is it, Perry?" Haversham asked.

That's his name, Tucker thought. *Perry.*

"Sorry to interrupt, sir," Perry said, and it irritated Tucker to realize he'd directed the *sir* toward Haversham, not him. "But Josiah Johnson's dead."

"Dead?" Tucker said. "Dead how?"

"Shot down in the street. And Tate's dead, too, sir."

"What are you telling me, Johnson and Tate shot each other?" Nobody had seen Tate for the better part of a week. Everybody figured he was off on another bender.

"No sir. Me and Josiah was in town getting the perfume you sent for, and Josiah looked over and saw Tate's horse, only it wasn't Tate who was unhitching him, it was some other man, so Josiah called out to him, and this man turned around, and they had words and drew, and the man shot him dead in the street."

"What about the perfume?"

The kid tilted his head like an idiot. "Sir?"

"The perfume I sent for. Where is it?"

"Shattered in the gunfight, sir. Josiah had it on him. He's dead, sir."

"You already said that," Tucker growled. Pearl was going to be mad about that perfume. She'd been complaining for weeks about having to wait. Now, he'd have to order it all over again, and she would probably refuse his affections until it arrived.

"You said Tate was dead as well," Haversham spoke up. "Is this merely conjecture on your part, or did you learn of this in Dos Pesos."

"The man who killed Josiah said he'd killed Tate. Well, he said Tate was dead and had sort of given him his horse or something like that, but you could tell that's how he meant it. And then he told Josiah to look at him, and Josiah said something about how it wasn't possible, how they had already killed him, and—"

"Killed Tate?" Tucker interrupted. He felt like grabbing this kid by the ankles and smashing his head off the big mahogany desk half a dozen times.

"No sir. Not Tate, sir. The other man. The one who killed Josiah. That's what Josiah said to him. That it wasn't possible. They had already killed him. He sounded scared half to death. Josiah, I mean. That other fella, he was about un-scared as anybody I ever saw. And quick? He was faster than fast. Josiah started to draw, and that was that. He was dead."

"I am interested to hear more about Josiah and the others having already killed this man," Haversham said, pushing his spectacles to the top of his nose. "What, exactly, do you think Josiah meant?"

Perry shrugged. "Gosh, sir, I don't know. It all happened so fast. I mean, one second, we was walking down the street, the next thing I know, Josiah was dead."

"Why didn't you shoot the man?" Tucker said.

"Sir?"

"Are you hard of hearing?"

"No sir."

"Tell me, then. How come you didn't shoot the man?"

Perry shook his head. "No way, sir. No way was that even possible. I mean, he was faster than a rattler riding a lightning bolt. He killed Josiah and turned his piece on me quicker than you could blink. Then the sheriff showed up and they carried Josiah off."

Tucker dropped into his chair and slammed a big fist down on the desk. "That Perkins is worthless. We need to give his badge to someone we can count on."

"Perhaps now is not the time," Haversham suggested, again with the aggravating smile. "We don't want to move too quickly. You remember what happened in Texas."

"Of course, I remember what happened in Texas!" Tucker thundered. "I lived it, didn't I?"

"You certainly did."

"What's that supposed to mean?"

Haversham spread his soft hands and smiled. "Only that it was a foolish question on my part, sir." The lawyer turned to Perry again. "Now, tell us everything you can remember about the man who killed Josiah."

Perry stumbled through his limited recollections, mostly repeating the same information, stressing again the man's height, eerie calm, and supernatural speed.

Haversham pushed up his spectacles again. "Josiah said 'we already killed you'?"

"Yes sir."

"Who was we?"

"I don't know, sir."

"Do you believe he was speaking of the late Mr. Tate and himself?"

Perry shrugged. "Could be, sir. They hung around together. Them and Del Mundo and Beachem."

"Yes," Haversham said, drawing out the word as if deep in thought. "Thank you, Perry. You did the right thing coming straight here and telling us everything."

"Yes sir. Thank you, sir," Perry said, speaking only to Haversham, as if Tucker wasn't even in the room.

"You may go now," Haversham said, "but Perry?"

"Yes sir?"

"Do send in Del Mundo and Beachem. I would like to speak with them."

"Yes sir."

Watching the boy leave, Tucker felt more irritated than ever. It wasn't Haversham's place to dismiss the nitwit, it was Tucker's.

But that was the least of his irritations.

Tucker had thirty men on his payroll. Until a few days ago a dozen of them could be trusted in a fight. Now, three of those men were dead: Tate, Josiah Johnson, and Cal Benner over at the cattle gate—Tucker still couldn't reckon what, exactly, had gone down there, but whatever had happened nobody disputed one fact: Benner was deader than a hammer.

So three of his reliable gunmen were gone, and two more were out of commission, thanks to that crazy Lopez woman.

Now, he only had Del Mundo, Beachem, and five other guns he could truly count on.

That was troubling.

He'd learned in life that things either went his way or went against him. Good luck and bad moved over him like slow-moving storms, dominating long periods and changing his life the way passing seasons changed the open range. When things were going right, everything went right. When they went wrong, look out.

Things had gone about as wrong as possible in Texas.

But then, all of a sudden, everything had turned up roses. He'd gotten the invite to visit Colorado, set up this New Mexico deal, and met Pearl over the course of a single week.

Now, though, it felt like bad was piling up on top of bad again.

Well, he wouldn't stand back and let his life fall apart. No sir. It was time to strike and set things right, starting with the Lopezes and then with this mystery man who gunned down Tate and Johnson.

In the meantime, his biggest concern was that perfume. Pearl would be furious.

He rose and started pacing again, wishing there was some way to just gather up the whole situation in his big hands and squeeze the life out of it.

"Shall I send for Mr. Rose?" Haversham asked.

Tucker quit pacing.

It was a tempting suggestion. Rose would quickly end his troubles with this mystery man and anyone else who needed killing, but calling for him would also make Tucker look weak.

If he wanted to make something of himself here in New Mexico, he needed to be strong, needed to look like he was completely in control.

Tucker was so close to having everything he ever wanted. Pearl loved the new house and was happier than he'd ever seen her. And more receptive as well.

If he messed up now and showed some belly, he'd be replaced, Pearl would lose the house, and then…

Well, he didn't know what exactly, but it wouldn't be good.

He couldn't allow that to happen.

He glared at Haversham. "No, we don't need Rose."

Haversham showed his irritating smile. "We cannot

ignore his man, whoever he is. He killed two of your employ-ees. He must be dealt with."

"You think I don't know that? We'll deal with him ourselves. Send Beacham and Del Mundo after him. Sounds like he's their business anyway. In the meantime, go to Dos Pesos and take care of the Lopez problem."

CHAPTER 16

Returning to the ranch Justice was greeted by Eli and Rafer. He patted both of them on the head and felt a surge of fierce protectiveness.

Until now, he had been operating in secrecy. But today he had shot a trigger-happy gate guard on a neighboring ranch and gunned down a bad man in plain sight on the same street where plenty of folks had seen him walking with Nora and Eli. Before long, Tucker would hear rumors placing Justice here at Nora's ranch.

And not just Tucker. Del Mundo and Beachem, too.

"Where did you get the horse, Justice?" Eli asked, admiring the strawberry roan trailing behind the bay.

"That's a long story," Justice said, figuring Nora might want to be the one to tell it, "but he's ours now."

From Josiah Johnson's horse he'd gained a Yellowboy rifle and saddlebags filled with jerky, two bottles of whiskey, and ammunition.

He let the horses drink, then led them into the stable where he removed the saddles and bags. "Throw down some hay, Eli. We'll give them some oats later after they've had a rest."

"Yes sir."

Eli did as he was told and watched as Justice rubbed down the horses, speaking gently to them.

"Can they understand what you're saying?" the boy asked.

"Some," Justice said. "Mostly, it's just my tone."

"Your tone?"

"The sound of my voice. The feel of it. You want to talk to horses calm and quiet. Makes a horse feel safe. But he'll trust me, too, so that also means I'm in control. It's important to know your animals and to make sure they know your voice. Horses, dogs, cattle. Even sheep, as dumb as they are. You let cattle mix, you got a day's work finding and cutting your cows. That's why you gotta brand them, especially on open range. But you mingle two flocks of sheep together, it's no problem. When you want to split them just call your sheep, and they'll come to the voice they know."

Eli looked amazed. "I never knew that."

Justice tousled the boy's hair. "Well, you're only six, son. I reckon there's plenty yet for you to learn."

They went inside where Nora had lunch waiting for them.

"I see a new horse and rifle," she said, eyeing the Yellowboy with concern. "What happened?"

"Plenty."

"Eli, go out and look through the tomatoes," Nora said. "Pick the two nicest slicers you can find. Now, take your time, you hear? I want to see if you can spot the two very best."

"Yes Mama." The boy scampered outside, clearly pleased by her challenge.

With the boy occupied Justice told Nora all about what had happened in town.

She had plenty of questions.

He answered all that he could until Eli returned.

Then they sat down to a delicious lunch of rice and beans, fresh tortillas, and thick slices of tomato.

"I have to give it to you, Eli," Justice said, smiling across the table at the little fellow. "You sure can pick a nice tomato."

Eli beamed like he'd just been crowned king of the Earth.

After they finished eating Justice sent Eli outside to give the bay and the strawberry roan a bait of oats.

"I reckon you and Eli ought to stay in town for a while. I have money. You can get a nice room in the hotel, have a hot bath every day, eat your meals at the restaurant, make a real nice time out of it. Just till this blows over."

"And leave you alone?" Nora said, crossing her arms.

"People saw me, Nora. Saw my face. Some of those same folks undoubtedly saw us together, too. Folks who know you, who know where you live. There could be real trouble."

She lifted her chin looking more determined—and to Justice anyway—more beautiful than ever. "You don't know me quite so well as I thought you did, Justice. I will not leave my house, and I will not leave you. If Tucker's men attack the ranch, I will stand and fight alongside you."

Justice nodded. "Your ranch, your choice. I wish you'd see things my way, but—"

"Save your breath," Nora said. "I've made up my mind. If I went away and something happened to you, I would never forgive myself. Not ever. I would rather die beside you than live with that guilt."

"All right," he said, his heart full of love for this woman, and once again, it was all he could do not to pull her into an embrace and kiss her. "But if you change your mind—"

"I won't. I have faith in you, Justice. When those men

killed you I prayed my heart out. First, I prayed for you. But then when I saw you were dead, I prayed for vengeance. That's when the lightning struck. God didn't just save you because I asked Him to, Justice. He saved you so you could do His work. He brought you back to destroy the wicked."

———

THE TWO OF THEM SAT ON DIEGO'S PORCH DRINKING lemonade, their rifles leaned against the rail nearby. A scrawny barn cat swiveled between Diego's boot and the leg of the chair.

Justice had explained everything.

Diego took it all in solemnly then offered to help the Lopezes by purchasing a few steers.

"Good," Justice said. "Mrs. Lopez will be pleased."

They sat in silence for a long moment, each man staring out at the sunbaked land beyond the home.

"I doubt Tucker wants a full-blown range war," Diego said.

"I don't know the man."

"Neither do I, but why would he want all that blood on his hands? He already owns half of the valley. Why risk it with a full-scale war? He's new to the territory. He pushes that hard, folks will rise up against him. He has to know that after what happened to him in Texas."

Justice rocked back on his chair legs. "Men do crazy things especially for money, land, or power, and all three are at stake for Tucker. There's no telling what he might do."

"Well, if he wants war, he'll get it. My boys will fight. Most will, anyway. A couple are untested."

"How big is Tucker's crew?"

Diego grinned. "Not as big as it was this morning."

"Yeah, there is that."

"I reckon he has thirty or forty men riding for him."

"Might hire more if he's gunning for a war."

"That he might. So what we gotta do is talk to our neighbors, just like somebody must've done back in Texas. I know Dave Fremont's had some cattle stolen, and old Chester Robinson is always ready for a fight. If you think Tucker's going to make a move, we best get organized now, not later, after it's too late."

"Good thinking."

"We'll ride over to Chester Robinson's place first. He'll be all fired up. But he is also fiercely independent. If we can get Chester to throw in with us, the others stand up and take notice. Mark my words. It'll be much easier to recruit the others if Chester joins us."

"I'm ready when you are."

"You're not much for wasting time, are you?"

"Never saw much use in it."

"Well, I reckon we'd best wait and visit tomorrow, or you might be late for dinner. I don't want Nora scalping me."

"All right."

"Speaking of Nora, you really can't talk her into staying in town?"

"Not a chance."

Diego nodded. "Well, maybe you could at least talk her into letting Eli stay with Eugenia and me for a spell. If anything happens out at your place…"

"I appreciate that, and I'll run it by Nora and see what she says."

Diego grinned slyly. "Boy stays here you might even want to quit sleeping in the barn."

Justice shook his head. "The barn suits me fine."

"You blind or just stupid?"

Justice laughed.

Diego looked at him seriously. "You remember something about your past?"

"No. But it's still there."

"Think you have a family somewhere?"

"I have no idea. Until I do know I can't in good conscience sink my roots here."

"You care for Nora, though, don't you? And the boy?"

"I love them both."

Diego nodded, seeming pleased. "I figured you did. She's a good woman, and he's a good boy. I'll be honest. They need you, Justice. And, if I may be so bold, I reckon maybe you need them, too."

Justice didn't say anything. The old rancher had taken size of everything, all right.

"Look," Diego said, "this is none of my business, but I'm going to have my say anyhow."

"I kind of noticed you have that way about you."

"Yeah, you get my age, you tend to speak your mind."

"Speak it then."

"I'm trying. If you'd quit chattering."

Justice chuckled.

"First of all," Diego told him, "I respect what you're saying. I mean, what you're doing, it's the decent thing to do. But the decent thing isn't always the right thing. What about death do us part?"

Justice cocked one eyebrow.

"That's what the preacher always says. A man and woman are bound in marriage until one of them dies. And from what I understand, you already died, my friend."

"Tell me something. If you went off and died then came back to life, would you abandon Eugenia, leave her to her own devices, let her spend the rest of her life thinking you were dead?"

Diego looked at him for a second. "No. No I would not."

Justice stood and handed Diego his glass. "Thanks for the lemonade. Tomorrow morning, after I help those men get settled over at the Lopezes, we'll go see this Chester Robinson. I might have a good idea about how to frame our request."

CHAPTER 17

"You men wait here," Haversham told Del Mundo and Beachem, "and stay out of trouble."

Haversham saw anger flash in the eyes of the hired guns, but they knew better than to question him.

He left them standing there and went inside.

"What can I do for you, Mr. Haversham?" Sheriff Perkins asked.

Haversham sidestepped a bloodstain. The blood had been sopped up, but it nonetheless darkened the floorboards.

He did not smell blood, however; he smelled familiar perfume... the same cloying stench he associated with the physically attractive yet utterly repulsive Mrs. Tucker.

He pushed up his spectacles staring down at the stain. "This blood once belonged to Josiah Johnson, I presume."

"You presume correct," Perkins said.

"And where is he now?"

"The undertaker's got him. You heard what happened?"

"Yes, that's why I'm here, of course. A brilliant deduction on your part. Which is why, no doubt, you are the shepherd of this town."

Perkins looked at him. His mouth couldn't quite decide whether to smile or frown. Ultimately, it wriggled, reminding Haversham of a dying caterpillar.

Haversham took a seat without being asked. "Tell me about him."

"Who, Johnson?"

"No," Haversham said, thinking again how fear turned men like Perkins into babbling idiots, "his murderer."

"Well, first of all, I wouldn't call the man a murderer. A lot of folks saw what happened. Every one of them says Johnson drew first. Or tried to, anyway. This other fella was too quick for him."

"Tell me about him." Haversham smiled as if he were dealing with a simple-minded child. "The one who's still living, I mean."

"I don't know him. Goes by Justice, that's all I know."

"A fascinating moniker. One could even call it ironic."

"Yeah." Perkins said, smiling sickly.

Haversham wondered if the sheriff even knew he was clutching his potbelly. "Where might I find this Mr. Justice?"

"Your guess is as good as mine, Mr. Haversham. Like I say, I don't know the man. Perhaps you'll find him down at the hotel."

"Perhaps. Before coming here I spoke with several of your sheep."

"My sheep?"

"Your townsfolk. A few of them told me something quite interesting."

"What's that? If they said I know him, they're liars."

Haversham smiled, having confirmed what he already suspected. Perkins did know the man. Or at least knew more than he was letting on.

Which surprised Haversham to some small degree. After

all, Perkins was clearly frightened. Why would he protect this man?

Did he actually know the man well?

No, Haversham didn't think so. If that were the case someone would have tipped him off.

Why, then? Why protect the man when his position as sheriff was on the line?

Could this Justice have offered Perkins something? A large sum of money, perhaps?

Doubtful.

Which left only one other possibility. And it seemed the obvious choice to Haversham.

Perkins feared this man. Feared him more, in fact, than he feared Haversham, Tucker, Del Mundo, Beachem, or losing his position.

Interesting.

On the ride in, Del Mundo and Beachem had scratched their heads, trying to figure out who the man might be. They ran through different folks they could remember shooting, but none of them seemed possible.

When Haversham told them to consider people they had actually killed, they grew more specific, rattling over half a dozen different unfortunates, including the lawman they'd dispatched on the banks of the river two or three months earlier.

Now, sitting across from the sheriff, Haversham thought. Lawman... *Justice*... Interesting.

Then he remembered the telegram Tucker had received from Colorado, the telegram that had initiated that killing. Could it be?

Something to investigate, certainly.

Outwardly, Haversham retained what he thought of as his professional smile. "Not to worry, Sheriff Perkins. No one alleged any connection between you and your Mr. Justice. They did, however, tell me that he had visited town before."

Perkins was visibly trembling now. "Yeah, that's right. Brought in Tate and collected the bounty. What of it?"

"Well, I'm certain Mr. Tucker would have appreciated an update concerning that development."

"Look, I'm sorry. I've been busy. And I was gonna let Tucker know. It's just—"

"Not to worry, Sheriff Perkins, not to worry. I was speaking of another occasion. I heard that Mr. Justice recently came to town in the company of a lovely woman."

Sheriff Perkins' eyes bulged slightly, but he tried to disguise his reaction with a shrug. "Lots of pretty women in these parts."

"This one is anglo. Blond hair, blue eyes. She had a young boy, a son of similar hair and eye color, with her that day."

Perkins made a show of scratching his head. "Sorry, Mr. Haversham. I don't know who that might be. But if I think of anything—"

"Not long ago I visited a beautiful blonde on Mr. Tucker's bidding," Haversham said, smiling. "Nora Eckert. Do you know her?"

Perkins shrugged again. "In passing, I suppose."

Once more, Haversham could see the man was lying. "Do you believe that our Mr. Justice could be at her ranch?"

"Again, your guess is as good as mine. Though I'd have to say I kindly doubt it. That Eckert woman's a godly widow, and I haven't heard of any marriages lately. I don't believe she would take up with a man outside of wedlock."

"One never can tell, though, can one? This Mr. Justice seems like a miracle worker. Perhaps I will look for him there. If nothing else, I should warn the Widow Eckert about the recent nastiness that transpired on a neighboring ranch. You heard of the unpleasantness at the Lopezes?"

Perkins looked sick again. "I heard about it. Terrible business."

"Indeed. Fortunately, Mr. Tucker is willing to step in and help the poor Lopez family."

"That's, er… very nice of him."

"Yes, it is, isn't it?" Haversham said, rising to his feet. "Mr. Tucker wants nothing more than to become a pillar of this fledgling community."

"That's good to hear, Mr. Haversham. Very good to hear. You have yourself a nice day and give my best to Mr. Tucker."

"Thank you, Sheriff. I will." He paused at the door and turned back to the quivering man. "And one more thing, Sheriff. If I ever discover you're holding back information from us, you will lose your badge faster than you can say *dereliction of duty*, do you understand?"

"Yes sir."

"Very well then, Sheriff. Carry on."

Haversham went out into the afternoon sun feeling pleased with the visit. He had a much better understanding of the situation now and suspected he could find this Mr. Justice at Nora Eckert's farm.

He also suspected that Mr. Justice might well be the lawman Tucker's thugs had gunned down by the river. After all, hadn't that transpired on Nora Eckert's property?

The question was, how much should he tell Tucker?

Generally speaking, Haversham played his cards close to the vest, especially where Tucker was involved.

Since no one was directly identifying Mr. Justice or his location, Haversham would likely sit on his own deductions for a time. That would allow him to observe how Tucker handled everything.

The man drank too much and worried too much about the opinions of his wife. He wasn't stupid, exactly, but he was highly emotional.

In fact, emotion was both Tucker's greatest strength and weakness. He was impulsive, brutal, and capricious. These traits both helped and hurt him on this raw frontier.

They had destroyed him in Texas, but here in the New Mexico Territory, they had made him almost a power broker. *Almost.* One day, Tucker might become a true power broker. He had certainly been given the opportunity.

But would Tucker reach greatness?

It was too early to tell. Many things could go wrong along the way.

Haversham, of course, would keep his distance if things did go south for Tucker. He had no interest in becoming a power broker himself, but he was a man accustomed to the finer things in life.

How he missed the restaurants of New York and Chicago. The opera. The delicate, milk-white ladies in their long dresses and sparkling jewelry. All of it.

But he had most unfortunately been run out of both towns and could not hope to go back—not, that was, without an enormous sum of money. After the scandals he would certainly never be allowed to practice law again.

That was okay. Haversham had little interest in the law now, save for how he might wield it to gain what he really wanted. He would not rest until he had extricated himself from this miserable frontier and returned to civilization, where those finer things could once more be his. He could all but taste the escargot, all but smell the lovely Cuban cigars, all but hear the flawless orchestras, all but feel the tender flesh of rich men's daughters in his squeezing hands.

He would have it all again.

If Tucker rose to real power, Haversham would rise alongside him and use that wealth to start over—this time in San Francisco, he believed. Apparently, their restaurants were quite impressive, and few there, if any, would know his face.

If, on the other hand, the blustering Mr. Tucker fumbled this situation and sunk into oblivion, Haversham would be poised to abandon him prior to being sucked into his wake.

For the time being, he would not report everything to Tucker. This mystery man might be the perfect catalyst to push Tucker either toward ruin or power. Either result could benefit Haversham, so long as he reacted properly.

In the meantime, he would fix the Lopez situation.

Haversham turned his attention to Del Mundo and Beachem, who were leering at passing women.

Men like these he had come to understand. They were primitive and dangerous, like half-tamed dogs. You could never let your guard down around them, never be friendly— men like Del Mundo and Beachem registered friendliness as fear—but you also couldn't push them too hard. The trick was to constantly remind them of your socially dominant position without sharply offending them, in which case they might impulsively murder you.

Oh, how he loathed the West.

"Stop ogling women and come with me," he snapped impatiently. "I have a job for you two."

CHAPTER 18

T he next day at midmorning nearing the Lopezes' ranch house, Justice figured the new hired hands would soon spot him.

He didn't know these men and didn't know what, precisely, Barrera had told them.

So he approached slowly.

Better safe than sorry. Getting shot wasn't at the top of his list of things to do today.

He was surprised to see not two men but a dozen on the ranch. Some rode among the cattle. Most were coming and going from the ranch house.

A laughing man ambled out of the door holding a woman's dress up to his dusty range clothes as if modeling it for the other cowboys.

Something wasn't right here.

Far from it, in fact.

He quickly scanned the group for a hulking redhead or black-bearded hunchback but saw neither and recognized no one. That being said, he had no doubt who these men rode for.

What was Tucker up to?

Justice kept coming, curious to the core.

At last, when he was seventy yards from the house, someone spotted him and gave a shout.

There was some commotion among the men. Finally, two of them rode out carrying their rifles unsheathed across their saddles.

Justice left his weapons holstered and offered what he hoped was a disarming smile.

The two riders drew within twenty feet and stopped their horses.

Behind them the other men watched. They hadn't pulled their shooting irons yet, but that could change in the blink of an eye.

Justice knew he couldn't shoot his way out of this. He could only talk his way back home.

"Who are you?" one of the men demanded.

Thinking quickly, Justice said, "Name's Bill Benson. Are you Mr. Lopez?"

"Do I look like Mr. Lopez?" the cowboy sneered.

"My apologies for not knowing your name," Justice said. "I was told I could find a Mr. Lopez here and that he might be willing to sell me some cattle."

"These cows is already bought, mister. They's the property of Mr. Sullivan Tucker, as is the ground where we're standing."

"Shucks," Justice said, shaking his head. "Tucker, you say? I was under the impression that a man named Lopez owned this ranch."

The cowpoke who'd been doing the talking grinned, showing a rack of stubby teeth stained brown with tobacco juice. He spat. "He did until yesterday afternoon. His woman sold every acre and all that was on it to our boss."

———

JUSTICE RODE TO TOWN THANKFUL NONE OF THE COWPOKES recognized the bay. Thankful, but not surprised. Most of them were a good distance off and all riled up, looting the place. And the Sullivan Tuckers of the world retained men like Tate and his associates for purposes other than roping and branding and riding herd, so these punchers might not have known Tate or his horse very well.

Besides, bays were common in these parts. If he'd ridden Johnson's strawberry roan, someone would have put two and two together.

He'd already ridden a good distance, so instead of tethering the bay outside the hotel, Justice visited the livery.

"You drop what you're doing and care for my horse now, I'll give you a full dollar to feed him and rub him down and run the curry brush over him," Justice told Manuel Chavez, the owner.

Chavez nodded. "This I can do. I know this horse, *señor*."

"He only came into my possession recently."

Chavez offered a slight smile. "Ah, so you are the one people are talking about, *el pistolero*."

"That's me. This man I got the horse from, Tate, he used to ride with a few others."

"Including the one you killed yesterday."

"Right."

"They are bad men. Not bad to their horses, you understand. But bad men."

"Yes, they are. Would you recognize the horses of the others?"

"*Si, señor*, I know these horses well. The men come to town to drink and visit the bordellos and sometimes to fight. They leave their horses with me."

"Tell me about them."

"The one they call Beachem rides a chestnut Morgan with two white socks in back. Del Mundo rides what is perhaps the finest horse I have ever seen, a black quarter horse over 16 hands. A beautiful horse and very fast, I believe, very durable, a horse to dream of. But hear me, they are both very bad men, señor. Watch especially the man Beachem. He is very quick with his pistol."

"Thank you for the warning," Justice said. "If I run into them at the same time, I'll shoot Beachem first."

Chavez's place was at the edge of town. Justice started up the street watching for any sign of these men or their horses.

Shortly after he reached the planks he passed The Traveler's Repose, one of the town's three bordellos.

"Come on in, handsome, and let me unload your wagon for you," a raven-haired girl called from the entrance.

"I'll take care of you for free looking like you do," a strawberry blonde offered.

Justice said nothing, just tipped his hat to these soiled doves and kept on walking.

When he reached the hotel he spoke with the clerk, a young man whose efforts at growing a mustache weren't yielding much success.

"Good afternoon, sir."

"Afternoon," Justice said. He dropped a quarter on the counter and pushed it over to the young man. "I'm hoping you can answer some questions for me."

The boy brightened at once, slipping the quarter into his pocket. "Yes, sir. How can I help you?"

"Are the Lopezes still here?"

"Yes sir. Room 211."

"Did Mr. Lopez join his family?"

"Yes sir. Late last night some men carried him over on a pallet. They had a time getting him up the stairs, but they managed it."

"All right then. How many visitors have they had?"

"Just one, sir. Yesterday afternoon. Very well-dressed. He looked like he might be a lawyer."

"Little guy? Anglo? Glasses?"

"Yes sir."

That would have been Haversham, Justice thought, and he reckoned the men at the ranch had told the truth. Tucker's lawyer had come here and purchased the place and everything on it.

"Did he have anyone with him?"

"No sir."

"Did he ask any questions?"

"Just like you, sir… were the Lopezes here, and what room." Then the boy seemed to remember something. "Oh, he did ask one other question. I thought it was odd."

"What's that?"

"He asked if the Lopezes had a window facing the main street."

Justice went upstairs and knocked, and Mrs. Lopez's voice asked who it was.

He told her and heard the lock move, and the door opened to reveal a puffy-eyed Antonia Lopez.

Roberto lay on the bed unconscious flanked by his daughters, who were no longer crying but looked completely wrung out.

"May I come in?" Justice asked.

"Yes, please. But I fear you will not wish to stay. Mr. Justice, I am sorry, but…"

She hesitated, obviously ashamed to have sold the ranch after he'd helped her and hired hands.

"You sold the ranch," he said softly, not wanting her to feel bad.

"Yes, señor."

"To Tucker."

She dropped her eyes and whispered, "Yes."

Justice nodded toward the bed. "How's Roberto doing?"

"Not bad for a man with many gunshot wounds. We are lucky."

That's one way to look at it, Justice thought. And probably the best way, given their options. But what he said was, "I'm glad to hear it."

"Mr. Justice, I am sorry for selling the ranch."

"That's your business, not mine," he said, "but I would be interested in knowing how it came about. Last I knew, you weren't interested in selling."

"Mr. Tucker offered a great deal of money." Leaking tears, she nonetheless forced a brave smile. "We will start over. Not here, though. Anywhere but here."

"Well, I'm happy you'll be all right. Life comes at you catty-corner sometimes and knocks you into a whole new county. I wish you the best." He touched his hat, ready to leave, but one of the girls spoke up.

"Tell him, Mama. Tell him the truth."

Mrs. Lopez looked briefly terrified and glared at the girl, meaning to silence her.

The girl, however, stood from the bed and lifted her chin. She was nearly as tall as her mother, probably fifteen or sixteen, and her eyes flashed with indignation. "Tell him about Haversham. He deserves to know in case the same happens to him."

Justice turned to Mrs. Lopez and waited.

She hesitated then said, "Mr. Haversham dresses well and has soft, clean hands, Mr. Justice, but he is a very frightening man. At first, he was friendly. He asked about my husband—Roberto was not here yet, you understand—and then he apologized for any misunderstanding. He assured us that the incident had nothing to do with Mr. Tucker. He said Mr.

Tucker heard about it and felt terrible and wanted to help us because we were his neighbors."

"And you believed him?"

She nodded. "I did. Mr. Haversham is a very good liar, very convincing. At last, I believed him and opened the door and invited him inside."

"And I guess that's when the other shoe dropped."

"He made the offer to buy us out. I told him we were not interested. He upped the offer. I said we were not interested at any price. But then..." She trailed off, clearly overcome with emotion.

Justice waited.

"Tell him, Mama," the daughter demanded.

"Mr. Haversham led me to the window."

Justice figured he knew what she was going to say before she said it, and furthermore now understood why Haversham had asked the desk jockey about their window arrangement.

Mrs. Lopez cast a haunted look at the window in question, clearly remembering a difficult moment. "He pulled the curtain aside and pointed across the street where two men waited in front of the barber shop. One of them never stopped moving. Almost like he was dancing. He had a thick black beard. The other man stood looking up at us, waiting for a sign from Mr. Haversham. It was the big red-haired man, the one who came to our home, the one you call Del Mundo. I was very frightened."

"I'm sure. What did they do?"

"Mr. Haversham let the curtain drop. He smiled again and said that if I did not sell the ranch to Mr. Tucker, he would give a sign, and the two men would go inside and... and..."

Justice patted her arm. "It's okay, ma'am. I got the picture. Don't you worry. You did the only thing you could've done. Best of luck with your new lives."

CHAPTER 19

"Mr. Justice," Barrera said as Justice entered the otherwise empty barber shop, "you appear to have little respect for *closed* signs."

"I saw you through the glass."

"And yet, you almost did not, for I nearly escaped before you could locate me. Ah, before I forget."

Barrera reached into his vest, retrieved a stack of greenbacks, and handed them to Justice. "You will find only twenty dollars. Hector and Jorge both reported to work this morning but were driven off by Tucker's men."

"Your kin didn't get hurt, did they?"

"No, nothing like that. But they rode out and back, so I gave them each a dollar for their trouble. I am, however, returning the two dollars you gave me as a finder's fee."

Justice peeled off two greenbacks and handed them back to Barrera. "Keep your money. You did what I asked. And I'm fine with Hector and Jorge each keeping a dollar. Where are they now?"

"Across the street in The Third Peso getting a beer. Which strikes me as a good idea. When I looked out and saw

Beachem hopping back and forth, I thought, Alfredo, you are a fool to be the only doctor in town, for who will be your doctor when these men shoot holes in you? But then they left, and I went home and drank. But now I see you, and again I am thirsty." He shook his head.

"Well, come on, then. I'm about to head over and talk to your kin. I'll buy you a beer."

"Thank you, but no thank you," Barrera said, setting a derby hat atop his head at a jaunty angle.

"Thought you said you were thirsty."

"I am. But I have changed my mind about getting a beer."

"Why's that?"

"No offense, Mr. Justice, but I have noticed that wherever you go, bullets seem to follow. And as I have said, if I get shot who will tend my wounds? Enjoy your beer, my friend."

Justice scanned for threats, saw none, and crossed the street to The Third Peso.

It was only midday, but a good number of people stood at the bar and sat at the tables. Two card games were underway, and saloon girls moved from table to table flirting and slipping onto men's laps.

Justice tried to figure out which men might be Hector and Jorge. His eyes settled on two tanned and dusty men at the bar with a strong resemblance not only to one another but also to Barrera.

Justice walked over and spoke to the older man. "Would you be Hector?"

The man sipped his beer and studied Justice for a second before speaking. "Who are you?"

"I'm the guy who hired you to work the Lopez ranch."

"That job wasn't all it was cracked up to be, but it bought us these beers, anyway. Come, join us."

Introductions were made. Hector wore a Colt and seemed both confident and competent.

His son, Jorge, was cut of the same cloth, right down to the Colt on his hip. He was around eighteen or nineteen, but Justice figured he'd been around.

The barkeep came over. "What can I do for you?"

Justice laid a quarter on the bar. "Beer. And another round for my friends. Keep the change."

Pleased, the barkeep went off to get their drinks.

"You're dropping money like a man who just got a big bounty," Hector said.

"Two, actually. One on a guy named Tate, the other on Josiah Johnson. You know them?"

Hector shook his head. "They rode in with Tucker from Texas. Jorge and I were on the trail when Tucker was hiring, or we would probably be punching for him now. So is that what you do?"

"What, cowboy?"

"No, kill men. You a bounty hunter?"

"I guess? At least lately. But all I'm looking to do is help a woman run her ranch. Trouble is Tucker wants the ranch."

"Tucker wants everything."

"So I understand."

"He got the Lopezes, huh? My cousin said Mr. Lopez was all shot to pieces. And then Tucker used Beachem and Del Mundo to scare the wife."

"Yeah, that's pretty much the size of it. I went over there to meet you, and Tucker's men said he'd bought it."

Hector took a drink and grinned. "They didn't recognize you, huh?"

Justice shook his head.

"Most of them, they aren't so dangerous, anyway. They might be able to shoot, but they're cowboys, not killers. Not like you."

"And you?"

Hector shrugged. "I can fight. So can Jorge. We've been around."

"Well, you still want a job?"

"Depends. What kind of job? We can fight, but that doesn't mean we're looking for a fight."

"Same thing as it would have been at the Lopezes. Ranch work. But yeah, there could be trouble. Probably will be. Rustlers, raids. I'm guessing sooner or later Tucker will try to run us off like he did the Lopezes."

"So we'd be working for you?"

Justice nodded. "There's no bunkhouse. I sleep in the barn."

"What do you think, Jorge? You like to sleep in a barn?"

The younger man shrugged. "We could do that."

"There isn't much of a herd," Justice said. "Just a dozen cows and steers and one bull."

"Longhorn or short?"

"Long."

"How's the bull?"

"Not bad… for a bull."

"Those longhorns are smart. People say they're easy, but you gotta watch them."

"Mostly I need help expanding the stable. Sure would be easier with the two of you."

"We can do that. But we want more money. Not for the carpentry. This is a dangerous job."

"I won't deny it. How much you want?"

"Three dollars a day."

"For both of you?"

"No. For each."

"I'll give you two dollars a day."

"Five dollars a day for both of us."

"That's a lot of money."

"Not if we get killed."

"Fair enough. Five dollars a day. Let's drink these beers and head over."

––––––––

As usual, Rafer and Eli greeted Justice when he got back to the ranch.

The dog held his tail high circling Hector and Jorge when they dismounted.

"Eli, tell your mama I've hired two men to help us out for the next few weeks."

"Okay, Justice," Eli said. "She's making pie!" With that, the boy scampered off.

Justice showed the men the property, the horses, and the mules. He pointed toward the river. "Cattle are out yonder. Ride out and have a look. I gotta talk to Mrs. Eckert."

"Okay," Hector said, then grinned. "Don't eat all the pie."

"I don't make promises I can't keep."

Hector laughed. He and Jorge rode off.

Justice went inside. The ranch house smelled like heaven. Three pies sat cooling on the counter.

"I guess women really can read men's minds," he said, inspecting the pies. "How'd you know I was hiring a couple of hands?"

"I didn't," Nora laughed. "They can share our pie. But I have to ask, what possessed you to hire them? We run so few cattle."

"They're Hector and Jorge, the men I hired to look after the Lopez place. I rode over there to meet them, and a bunch of cowboys told me Tucker had bought the place."

"Oh no. I thought you said the Lopezes were staying."

"That's what they told me… yesterday. But a single day can change everything."

"You can say that again. What happened?"

He explained how Haversham had intimidated the Lopezes into selling.

"And you reckon he's coming for us soon?" Nora asked. "That's why you hired these men?"

Justice nodded. "That and to help me build. But yeah. Sooner or later, Tucker's going to test us. Right now, I have plenty of triggers but not enough fingers. These men'll help us defend against rustlers or worse."

"A smart move, Justice. How much do I owe them?"

"Nothing. They work for me. I have enough to employ them for a few weeks if need be."

"Well, thank you. I'll sleep easier."

"Happy to do it. And I'll sleep easier, too. Now, about these pies. Why are Hector and Jorge sharing our pie if you made three?"

"The other two pies are spoken for. You and Diego are still riding over to Chester Robinson's this afternoon, aren't you?"

Justice nodded. "Figured I'd head over to Diego's once I got Hector and Jorge settled in. I'll probably mark things out and have them get started digging holes for the corner posts."

"Well, they say you catch more flies with honey than vinegar. You bring Chester Robinson news of the range war, he might agree to ride with you against Tucker. Or he might decide to let you all settle your differences then take measure of the situation. But if you bring him one of these pies, I guarantee he'll see the light."

"Pretty confident of your pies, aren't you?"

"With good reason," Nora said with a smile. "I bake a good pie."

"That you do. But if we're eating one, and we're taking one to Chester, who'd you make the third pie for?"

"Eugenia. After all, she'll be watching Eli while I go to Chester's with you and Diego."

Justice grinned. "I've never met anyone quite like you, Nora Eckert. So you're coming with us, huh?"

"That's right. This is my property, and Chester likes me. He's an old widower, and I don't think he gets much pie. With me along the old soldier will see this as a matter of chivalry."

CHAPTER 20

The old battler Chester Robinson was as lean and hard and gray as seasoned ironwood. His long mustache drooped to either side of his mouth like a silver frown.

He acknowledged Diego with a subtle nod and eyed Justice cagily.

Seeing Nora, however, he straightened and smiled with surprising warmth then swept his hat from his head and bowed deeply.

"Mrs. Eckert, it is a profound pleasure to see you again."

"Likewise, Mr. Robinson. I hope you like pie."

"I love pie. And please, call me Chester. Now, where are my manners? You see what comes of being a widower for too long?"

Chester invited them onto the porch, took the pie inside, and returned with drinks, tea for Nora and whiskey for the men.

Nora retained her natural warmth but wasted no time before launching into the reason for their visit.

Justice and Diego had planned on doing their best to

wrangle the old rancher into seeing things their way, but Nora took the lead and did most of the talking.

Despite his reputation as five feet of barbed wire stretched across a ten-foot gap, Chester Robinson warmed instantly to Nora.

Justice was impressed to watch and listen as Nora made their case. She stuck to the truth using the facts of her situation, not melodramatic musings to sway the man, and Justice respected her for that.

By explaining her vulnerability she indeed awakened Chester's powerful sense of chivalry. Justice figured the old scrapper was ready to charge the gates of Hell with a bucket of ice water.

Then she explained the overarching situation, starting with how she had come to know Justice and explaining briefly what had happened with Tate and Johnson.

Chester regarded Justice with new respect.

Nora wrapped up by telling how Tucker had seized the Lopez ranch.

Chester spat over the rail. "That prissy little dandy boy of Tucker's has come here a couple of times. I told him to get off my property or I'd feed him to the pigs." He chuckled. "That made his baby blues fill up them spectacles of his. All right. I hear y'all. I reckon you're courting me for something. You want me to ride against Tucker, is that it?"

"Maybe," Justice said, "and yes, truth be told, it'll probably come to that. Seems like Tucker's bound and determined to take the valley, even if he has to kill all of us."

"Well, he's gonna have to kill me before he'll get an acre of my land," Chester said.

"Likewise," Diego said. "What we're thinking of doing is forming a cattleman's association."

Chester made a face like he'd just bitten into a rotten lemon. "I've never had much use for committees or associations. They say two heads are better than one, and maybe they are, but you put four or five heads together somebody wants to ride herd on the lot every time."

"This isn't that kind of association," Justice said.

"So you say."

Justice turned his eyes on the hard old man and let silence reign for a few seconds. He wasn't threatening the man or trying to intimidate him, but he was sending a message about who he was and letting Chester know that he expected to be taken seriously. "You calling me a liar?"

"Nobody's calling you a liar. I'm just waiting to hear what you mean by not that kind of association. I'm not much for rules and regulations, and I don't need anybody telling me what I can and can't do."

"Again, this will not be that kind of association. All we want to do is band together for the common defense and let Tucker know that if he tries pushing any of us, he'll have to answer to all of us."

"See, that makes sense to me. Why bother with an association at all? Let's just ride over there and put him in his place."

"By calling it an association," Nora said, "we legitimize ourselves."

"In whose eyes? I don't care what Tucker thinks."

"Neither do we," Diego said. "But I reckon Tucker cares what the territory thinks of him. He's a big thinker with big plans. It's not all about land and cattle, I'm betting. A man like Tucker, he wants to be a big shot in the territory. If we ride in there and tell him how it is and things get out of hand, he'll put a spin on it. Best case scenario the papers will say it's a range war. Worst case scenario they'll say a bunch of wild locals tried to run off an honest newcomer. The governor sure wouldn't like that."

Chester nodded. "I see what you're saying."

"If we create a cattleman's association, however," Justice said, "then go to Dos Pesos and file an official complaint with Sheriff Perkins—"

"Pshaw! Perkins is afraid of his own shadow! I wouldn't count on him to protect my chicken coop from a lazy fox."

"Agreed. But if we form the association and lodge an official complaint, the papers can't make us sound like a bunch of wild vigilantes. And Tucker will know that. The fight might be over before it even starts."

Chester grinned wolfishly. "Let's hope not. I haven't had a good fight in a long while."

By the end of their visit, the feisty old timer had signed the paperwork Diego's lawyer had drawn up earlier that day. It was a simple enough document, merely declaring that members respected one another's rights and were willing to help in the common defense. Most of the legalese actually dealt with what the association wasn't and couldn't do.

"I sure am glad you came along," Justice told Nora as they rode ahead of Diego on their way to the next ranch. Justice drove the wagon and Nora sat beside him, maintaining a gap of decency on the seat between them. "Thank you for winning him over."

Nora beamed at him. "Glad I could help. With the Gomezes it'll be best to let Diego do most of the talking. Mr. Gomez is an older gentleman, a *Nuevomexicano*, and a patriarch among patriarchs. He wouldn't trust you and wouldn't appreciate my speaking up."

Justice nodded, glad she knew her neighbors.

"Junior Martin will shout and strut," Nora said. "We'll let Diego start, but Martin views himself as the cock of the walk, and he won't sign on unless he thinks you can take him."

Justice laughed. "You want me to shoot him?"

"No, just be yourself. Once he gets through his obligatory blustering, he'll quickly take measure of you. Plenty of men have a touch of Martin in them. They need to pound their chests a little and have their say, but if they believe in a man and a mission, they will follow him regardless of the dangers."

It was nice spending this time with Nora. Eli was a joy, of course, but Justice enjoyed having this big block of time alone with Nora.

She was quite a woman. Not just beautiful and well-formed but also intelligent and hardworking, caring and perceptive, humble and humorous.

Justice enjoyed their conversation but also appreciated the calm stretches between the talking where they both rode along, perfectly content to pass time together without having to speak at all.

Regardless of any commitments to which he might still be held, he knew there could be no other woman in the world so perfect for him as Nora. In fact, it seemed to him then that she was the only woman in the world for him, the only woman he could possibly desire or cherish.

It was all he could do not to put an arm around her shoulders and draw her close.

Nora felt the same way and then some.

Unlike Justice, she was not hobbled by a shadowy past. Her own past was an open book, and she knew its contents chapter and verse.

Blake's death had released her from any commitment. She was a free woman. She loved Justice more than she could have ever dreamed of loving a man and wanted nothing more than for him to marry her and become Eli's second father.

If that came to pass she felt that nothing in this world— not scorching heat, drought, or the threat of men like Tucker —would ever daunt her again. With Justice she felt safe and happy and right.

Nonetheless, she respected and appreciated his restraint, even if half of her wanted him to cast it aside in favor of a life with her.

Ultimately, he was doing the right thing. She had to trust in the Lord and hope that she and Justice would be able to have a sanctified life together.

In the meantime, she simply sat there loving every moment, practically trembling with happiness and desire, thankful for this man having come into her life.

CHAPTER 21

Over the next week they visited two dozen small ranchers and made their case. It helped being able to share the signature of Chester Robinson, and by the time they had completed their circuit, sixteen ranchers had signed on.

Justice figured half of the holdouts, including the blustering Junior Martin, would soon join them, too. The frontier was a hard place, much farther from polite civilization than anything measurable in mere miles, and men strong enough to stake and defend a claim upon it tended to be suspicious, strong, and fiercely independent.

Justice couldn't blame them. He had a wide streak of those qualities himself.

Diego's lawyer, David Spencer, notarized the paperwork and promised to file a copy with the courthouse, along with an application that would legitimize the River Valley Cattleman's Association in the eyes of the territory and the law.

That was good enough as far as Justice was concerned.

Hiring Hector and Jorge turned out to be a great decision.

They earned every penny despite their high salary, seeing to the small herd of cattle and various chores around the ranch while focusing primarily on expanding the stable.

Hector had a good deal of carpentry experience, and Jorge listened well and learned quickly.

When he wasn't visiting other ranches, Justice worked alongside the men enjoying their company, and at night they took turns standing watch while the others bedded down in the barn. Justice took his turn on watch, too, and slept better with a guard posted at all times.

He was mildly surprised that Tucker's raiders hadn't tested the ranch. Nor had they attacked any of the other ranchers.

Sooner or later, however, they would strike, he knew. Here, elsewhere, everywhere.

And when they did the response of the River Valley Cattleman's Association would either embolden or discourage Tucker and men like him, affecting the future of the whole region.

Justice took time to practice with his weapons. He was already highly proficient with every firearm he touched, but that didn't stop him from practicing his quick draw every day, again and again and again.

"Whatcha doing, Justice?" Eli wanted to know one day when Justice stood behind the barn, outdrawing invisible opponents.

"Practicing."

"You sure are fast."

"I want to be faster. There is no second prize in a gunfight."

"I'll bet you're already faster than anybody in the whole world."

"Well, I don't know about that, son. I'd best keep practicing anyway. You never know when two men might draw on you at the same time."

The boy's mouth dropped open. Suddenly, he was offended as only a pure-hearted child could be. "That's cheating!"

Justice chuckled, reminded of the boy's youth. It's easy to forget sometimes, when you spend a good deal of time with a smart child, how intelligence is not the same as hard experience.

Part of him wanted to launch into a life lesson right then, explaining how fairness and rules of conduct went out the door as soon as a fight began; but he didn't want Eli blinding neighbor kids the next time they got into an argument, so he left it at, "Yeah, it is, so I'd better be ready, hadn't I?"

One day after Justice showed Jorge the basics of fighting with a Bowie knife, Hector retreated into the barn, saying, "I will show you what you need, my friend."

Hector came back out carrying the pipe tomahawk Justice had noticed hanging from the cowboy's saddle.

Hector handed it to him. "Ever use one of these?"

Justice hefted the weapon testing its balance. It felt perfect in his hand. "Truthfully, I don't know, but it feels downright familiar."

After two weeks of working side by side, the men knew about Justice's missing past, so his response was taken in stride.

Twirling, he swung his arm and released the tomahawk, which shot away in a tumbling trajectory and thwacked loudly into a corral post forty feet away. The blade was sunk deep in the wood.

"I think maybe he's used one before," Jorge laughed.

Meanwhile, freed by the help of Justice and the two hired hands, Nora used the slate and chalk Justice had gotten Eli to accelerate the boy's lessons, going from reading and reciting the alphabet to writing it and sounding out basic words.

When Eli worked alongside the men, Nora prepared the day's meals and saw to various tasks she had been largely neglecting since Blake's death, including sprucing up her home, mending old clothing, making new outfits, and getting caught up with her letter writing.

No sooner had she posted her first barrage of mailings than she received a letter of her own.

When Justice came inside that afternoon he found Nora reading the letter, smiling through tears.

"What is it?"

"My sister Mary in Santa Fe is about to give birth to her first child. My mother and a few of my sisters are coming to help her through it."

"That's wonderful news."

Nora nodded. "It truly is. Mary and I were always close. I feel bad for having drifted apart."

"I reckon you're being a tad too hard on yourself, Nora. You've been somewhat busy."

"I suppose. But I sure do wish I could be there for her."

"Let's go then."

"What?"

"Let's go to Santa Fe. I'll escort you and Eli there, and you can stay a while and help her with the baby."

"You're serious?"

"Of course. Let's go."

"But the ranch…"

"Hector and Jorge can hold down the fort while you, Eli, and I will go to Santa Fe. Then I'll come back and pitch in here."

She bit her lip. "A trip like that would be expensive."

"We can swing it, thanks to the bounty money."

"Oh, Justice, that would be wonderful!"

"It's decided then. Quit darning those socks and start packing. I'll ride into Dos Pesos, check tomorrow's stage schedule, and reserve three tickets."

Suddenly, Nora threw herself against him, laid her face on his chest, and wrapped him in a fierce embrace. "Oh Justice, you make me so, so happy."

"You make me happy, too, Nora. So very happy."

CHAPTER 22

S heriff Pat Perkins fastened his bib, inhaled deeply, and let his eyes flutter shut as the aroma of steaming buffalo stew filled his flared nostrils. His stomach grumbled in response wanting to be warm and full and heavy.

These were the moments Perkins lived for now: a nice bowl of stew, a cup of hot coffee, and an occasional pipe of good tobacco, which he picked up during his infrequent trips to Santa Fe.

He did not stoop to the vices of other men such as drunkenness, consorting with scarlet ladies, or gambling. Doing so would not befit a sheriff, though of course he knew plenty in his profession bothered with no restraint concerning these matters.

Perkins, however, held himself to a higher standard as the enforcer of law in Dos Pesos.

Unfortunately, he had never married and had no children, sweetheart, or even a dog to keep him company.

He'd had a cat for a while, but one day the tabby quit showing up, and Perkins assumed she'd gotten killed. Cats lead violent lives, after all, and die violent deaths.

If Perkins had one goal it was to avoid dying like a cat. He had never fully conceptualized this, of course, never put it into so many words even in his own mind; but his every move as sheriff touched and attempted to perpetuate this goal.

In some ways, this focus on self-preservation made him a better lawman. He was, for example, both cautious and hesitant to escalate any potentially violent situation.

But in other ways, this proclivity for self-preservation made him a far inferior lawman. If gunshots rang out like they had a short time ago between Josiah Johnson and the tall and terrifying Mr. Justice, Perkins made sure the echoes had died off before heading outside to investigate.

That preserved him to see to his second goal in life, which was the enjoyment of moments just like this one, when he was all bibbed up and ready to dive into a scrumptious meal.

He smacked his lips almost tasting the delicious stew already, opened his eyes, and gave a startled shout.

A man stood before his desk.

And not just any man.

A short, black-bearded man, shorter still for his hunched posture, rocking from side to side, twitching and sneering and staring at Perkins with obvious contempt.

Perkins had never even heard him open the door.

"Mr. B-B-Beachem," Perkins said, hating the cowardly stammer in his voice. "Is there a problem?"

"You tell me, Sheriff, is there a problem?" Beachem walked across the room, placed his hands on the desk, and leaned menacingly forward. "What have you done about the man who killed my friend?"

"I haven't seen him again. I... I think he left the territory. Afraid of you and Mr. Del Mundo, no doubt."

Beachem twitched then threw back his head and cackle-squawked like a dying rooster. "Afraid? The way I hear tell, he's hunting us.

"I can't imagine anyone hunting you, Mr. Beachem."

"Funny thing for a lawman to say."

"I only speak the truth. Everyone knows you're the fastest gun around."

"I hear this murderer is plenty fast himself. That's what everybody's talking about, how fast he is."

"I never saw him draw. He sure beat Johnson, though."

"My horse could outdraw Johnson."

"He took out Tate, too."

"Tate was too dumb to live. If brains were dynamite, Tate wouldn't have enough to blow his nose."

"Well, like I say, I think this man fled the territory. I doubt we'll ever see him again."

"Yeah, we will. He wants to face Del Mundo and me. And let me tell you, that's a wish he's gonna get."

"Who is he to you?"

"How should I know? I never seen the man."

"People say that Johnson claimed that he and some others already killed this man. They say Johnson was almighty frightened, like he was facing a ghost."

"Ghosts don't shoot people. What else do you know about this man?"

"Nothing."

"Bull. You talked to him, didn't you?"

Perkins nodded, wishing he wasn't wearing his bib. Suddenly, it made him feel like a big baby with a beard.

"Spill then," Beachem demanded. "Tell me what you can."

"Well, he's tall. Real tall. One of the tallest men I ever saw."

"Good. There's more of him to poke holes in. What else?"

"I don't know. Brown hair, kind of chestnut colored, I guess, but clean shaven the last time I saw him. Big, square jaw. Green eyes. Real bright green. He doesn't look like anybody you'd want to mess with."

Beachem's eyes flashed with a dangerous light. "You saying I'm afraid of him?"

Perkins's guts wobbled with terror. He just wished he could close his eyes, make Beachem disappear, and get back to his stew. "No, of course not. Not at all."

"I'm the fastest draw in this territory!" Beachem roared, and with a quick twitch he drew his weapon, reached across the table, and poked Perkins in the belly.

Perkins gasped and put his hands in the air.

"I got half a mind to pull the trigger and see what you had for breakfast."

"You can't."

Beachem twitched, eyes flashing. "Can't?"

"Shouldn't. I'm a lawman."

Beachem stared at him for a few seconds that stretched on and on and on. Then the hunchback threw back his head with another wild cackle. "A lawman!"

Beachem laughed and laughed then abruptly turned and crossed the room.

Perkins sighed.

Beachem stopped at the door and lifted his pistol, pointing again at Perkins, who raised his hands as if to shield himself... a foolish, cowardly motion, he instantly knew, but he still couldn't bring himself to lower his hands. "Wait. Don't."

"Listen to me, lawman." The way Beachem drew out lawman, he made it sound like the worst insult imaginable. "Mr. Tucker ain't happy. You want to keep this pitiful job, you'd best start keeping us apprised of things. You hear me?"

Perkins nodded.

"Now, if you were even half a lawman, you'd be out

hunting the man who killed my friends. Doesn't it concern you, a murderer running free in your jurisdiction?"

"It does. I... I'll start—"

"Spare me, Perkins. You sit here and eat your slop. I just got back in town today. Otherwise, I would've already outdrawn your tall stranger. I'm gonna take care of him for you, you hear? I'm going to shoot him down in the street like the no good dog he is. And that'll put to rest any of this claptrap about him being a quick draw. I'm going over The Cistern to get me some whiskey. You run into the murderer, send him my way, and we'll just see who's fast."

Beachem slipped from the office leaving the door ajar.

All at once, Perkins started shaking like crazy. For a moment, he just sat there paralyzed with fear.

He'd been so scared, so very scared.

Beachem was a demon.

Perkins sat there trembling trying to draw a full breath, and stared at the open door.

When at last the worst of the trembling had left him, he rose and crossed the room and shut the door, then walked back and fell heavily into his seat where he stared down at the thick brown stew, too defeated even to take a bite.

CHAPTER 23

Meanwhile, Beachem strode down the boards toward The Cistern. As usual, he walked quickly, taking a longer step with one leg than the other, which gave him the odd, hitching gait that made people notice him.

Up and down the boards people stepped aside making room for him. Those who recognized him muttered oaths and retreated inside.

Idiots, he thought. What did they think he was going to do, kill them all?

Not that he would mind.

In fact, that would be a hoot. Just ride in here someday and kill everyone. You'd need a pretty big crew for something like that, but you'd make a score, too, what with the stores and the bank.

Trouble was, if you rolled a whole town, all the real lawmen would come gunning for you. And considering the army you'd need to raze a town the size of Dos Pesos, the federal government might come down on you, too.

That was the last thing he needed, a regiment of cavalry riding after him.

Not that Beachem actually considered attacking the town. This was just the way his mind worked. He'd see something that triggered his thoughts, and they'd hop from one thing to another, often leaving a sizeable body count in their wake.

In reality, he cared only about killing one person at the moment, and that was the tall stranger who'd gunned down Tate and Johnson.

Not that Beachem cared about those two scoundrels. Neither one of them was worth the boots they were buried in.

Nor did he view this mysterious stranger as any real threat.

Two dozen times Beachem had drawn his pistol on other men, and two dozen times he'd walked away unscathed. Sure, a lot of those men he'd shot in the back, but a few he'd faced man to man, and they were dead and dust now.

Point was he'd done his share of killing and he was ready to kill this so-called killer, too.

Johnson's last words had rattled folks, principally Del Mundo, who seemed to think the tall man was someone they'd already killed; someone who'd returned from the grave to exact revenge.

Bunch of bunkum.

One thing Beachem had noticed: men he'd killed had a knack for staying dead.

Del Mundo thought it might be the one they strung up in the tree, the lawman.

That man had been tall. Beachem would give him that. But he'd also been dead. No pulse whatsoever.

And Beachem hadn't believed in ghosts since he was knee high to a grasshopper.

He pushed through the batwing doors of The Cistern and looked around with a snarl.

Men looked up wide-eyed at the sight of him, and conversation ebbed. The piano player missed a beat, then hurried on with his song.

Conversation returned albeit in hushed tones, men eyeing Beachem warily, paying him the respect he was due.

Beachem went to the bar.

The bar dog stopped what he was doing and poured Beachem a mug of beer with a frosty head, just like he liked it.

"Afternoon, Mr. Beachem," the bartender said. "Always a pleasure, sir."

Beachem took the beer without a word and started across the big room toward his table. He was in a foul mood. A killing mood.

Oh, how he hoped the tall man came to town today. Came to town and walked in here.

If not, Beachem would come back the next day. And the day after, if necessary.

Because this was personal.

Again, not because of those idiots Tate and Johnson. They were dead weight to begin with.

No, this was personal because folks kept saying how fast the tall man was, when they all should've known who was the fastest draw in the New Mexico Territory.

Beachem.

It kindly irked him, them even speaking in those terms, as if any man could come close to his speed.

Well, he'd remind them all right. And once he'd gunned down this pretender, there wouldn't be any more gibberish about fast draws.

Harvey Beachem was the only fast draw in these parts, and he wouldn't suffer any pretenders to live.

He remembered when Tucker had sicced them on the lawman. The orders had come down from on high. Or at least higher up. Either Colorado or Mexico, Beachem thought.

Honestly, he'd heard little and cared less. But they said the lawman was riding their way, supposedly following some lead Tucker's boss didn't want him chasing.

Tucker turned Beachem, Del Mundo, Tate, and Johnson loose on him and told them to send a message with no signature.

They figured the lawman would spend the night in the old barn in Burnt Crossing, so when they arrived there late that night, they stopped short of the burned-out farm and sneaked up close, and sure enough, a horse was picketed outside the barn.

Beachem had wanted to take him then, but the other men were afraid to face him.

Del Mundo tried to play it off, saying he wanted to get information out of the man. Lot of good that did them.

When the lawman came out of the barn the next morning, Del Mundo smashed him in the back of the head with the butt of his Winchester, and the tall man had dropped like a sack of bones.

They stripped his weapons and put the boot leather to him.

Then when the lawman came to again, Del Mundo made a show of questioning him, asking him what he was up to and where he'd been and who was hiding money around these parts.

But the lawman didn't say two words, no matter how much they beat him. He was stubborn, that was for sure. They could've skinned him alive, and he wouldn't have even told them his name.

So they'd dragged him behind Del Mundo's horse and then beat him some more before stringing him up.

Everybody was riled up on account of he was supposed to

be some special type of lawman, a "silent justice," like the ultimate hombre. But once again, people's talk amounted to so much dung. Killing their big lawman had been easier than taking off your boots on a hot day.

In fact, Beachem hoped Del Mundo's fears were right. He hoped it was the famous lawman they'd killed. Because man or ghost, Beachem would send him straight back to the grave.

He finished the first beer quickly and wiped a forearm across his mouth. Before he'd cleared the foam from his whiskers, the barkeep was setting another beer on his table.

"Keep 'em coming," Beachem growled and rubbed his thumb back and forth over the hammer of his Colt.

CHAPTER 24

J ustice rode the strawberry roan into Dos Pesos, pleased
with the horse and the general state of things.

He was happy with the progress on every front,
from the work he was doing with Hector and Jorge to the
way the River Valley Cattleman's Association was coming
together and especially the impending trip with Nora. She
was clearly excited to see her sisters and mother, and seeing
Nora happy made him happy.

Beyond that happiness, however, he had mixed feelings
about visiting Santa Fe. It was a big town, one folks in the
territory tended to visit sooner or later.

Was he from Santa Fe? Or a frequent visitor? Would
people there know him? Was tomorrow the day he would
uncover his hidden past?

The notion twisted his guts. Yes, he needed to recover his
lost life, but he did not want to lose Nora and Eli.

Coming into town he pushed those thoughts from his
mind. He couldn't change his fate by dwelling on it, and
nothing good ever comes from worrying.

He stopped by the livery and left his horse with Manuel

Chavez, not knowing how long his various errands would take him.

He went to the stage station, checked the schedule, and learned a coach would indeed be leaving for Santa Fe the next morning.

He reserved three seats, paying in advance, and then dropped in on Diego's lawyer, David Spencer.

"Good to see you again, Mr. Justice," Spencer said. "What can I do for you today?"

"I wanted to check and see how things were coming with that paperwork."

"Couldn't be better. Everything is officially notarized and filed with the courthouse, and your application has been processed and approved."

"That was fast."

"Indeed. The powers that be smile upon such associations."

"They get their filing fees."

"Yes, but beyond that, they believe such organizations strengthen law and order in the territory."

"Well, I hope they're right."

"Whatever the case, congratulations. You're now a member of the official River Valley Cattleman's Association."

"Thank you, but I'm actually not a member. Nora, Diego, and the others will be pleased, however."

"Excellent. I also investigated your other request, and the newspaper will be happy to run the full-page announcement you mentioned for eight dollars. Knowing you wanted to see to this quickly, I drew up some text. Would you care to read it?"

"Please."

Spencer handed him a sheet of paper announcing the River Valley Cattleman's Association, listing its members, and stating these ranchers had bonded together in goodwill and common defense against rustlers and violent criminals. At the end Spencer had declared, *"An attack on any will be answered by all."*

Justice handed the sheet back to the lawyer, who said, "Anything you'd like to add, delete, or change, just let me know and—"

Justice waved him off. "No, it's perfect as is, Mr. Spencer. I appreciate it." He took out his wallet and handed Spencer the eight dollars for the full-page ad.

"Outstanding, Mr. Justice. I will do everything I can to get this into tomorrow's paper."

After leaving the lawyer's office, Justice went next door to the Dos Pesos Bank, where he opened a bank account with both his name and Nora's on it. For the time being, he only deposited ten dollars, but he was happy to have the dual account in place.

That way if something happened to him, Nora could still access his money, and if he did uncover his past and it led him elsewhere, he would still be able to wire Nora and Eli money from time to time. Regardless of what he discovered, he would never stop caring about or helping them. He would sooner die than forsake them.

Leaving the bank he went up the street, figuring he'd tell Sheriff Perkins about the new cattleman's association. It was time to call Perkins's bluff.

As he approached, however, he noticed a chestnut Morgan with two white socks tethered outside Perkins's office.

Justice laid a hand on the butt of his Colt and opened Perkins's door but was disappointed to see no sign of Beachem.

"Oh no," Perkins said from behind his desk. His bib sat beside an untouched bowl of stew. "Just when I thought this day couldn't get any worse. Look, Justice, you'd better get out of town... fast."

"Where is he?"

"Down at The Cistern hoping you'll show up. He says he's going to kill you."

"He's wrong. I'm gonna kill him. Now look, Perkins, things are coming to a head with Tucker. The small ranchers have thrown in together and formed a cattleman's association. We went through a lawyer, filed our paperwork, and paid our fees, and it's official. We are a recognized entity formed for the mutual defense of our persons and property."

Perkins's eyes bulged as if he'd swallowed his spoon.

"The time for straddling the fence is over, Perkins. You gotta choose a side."

The sheriff shook his head. "I reckon I might just surrender my badge and hang up my gun."

"If that's what you need to do, do it. But don't kid yourself. You do that, you'll never stop running."

Perkins blinked at him.

"Instead of running, stand with us. We're going to ride over to Tucker's and tell him to mind his manners. Ride with us."

"Don't go stirring up a range war. What happened over in Lincoln County was a certified travesty."

"We don't want a range war. We want law and order. We are riding over there in a show of force to avoid a war."

Perkins looked sick to his stomach. "What exactly do you mean by *a show of force?*"

"Depends on how Tucker receives us. We're not gonna play it like he does, if that's what you're asking. We're not gonna ride over there unannounced and start shooting everyone and stealing his cattle in the middle of the night. But we are going to show him that we're united. Show him that a bunch of men with rifles and shotguns are willing to stand up to him. And if they fire on us, we will do more than stand up, we'll fight back."

Perkins clutched his gut and frowned.

"But listen, we want you with us," Justice said. "We've been careful to do everything legally. We're riding on the side of law and order. Having you along with us will make a big statement. It'll legitimize our cause."

"It'll get me fired... or killed."

"You're the sheriff, Perkins. You gotta do this."

"I don't know."

"Well, it's time to choose. We're announcing the association in the paper, and in a few days we're going to ride over there and tell Tucker how it is. If you don't ride with us, you'd best turn your badge over to someone who's man enough to do his job."

Perkins dropped his eyes and stared into the congealing stew as he shook his head woefully. "I'll let you know. But hey, Justice. You've tarried long enough. You'd best get out of town before it's too late. Beachem's already been down to the saloon for an hour. He might come out and spot you."

"He doesn't have to come find me. I'm going to go see him right now."

"Don't do it. He's the fastest draw around, and he's a stone-cold killer, Justice. He says he's gonna gun you down like a dog. I never like to see you coming, but I don't want to see you dead, either. Get on out of here while you still can. If you're going to face Beachem, face him with all of your friends."

"No can do, Perkins. I'm not the type of man who likes to put off work. Beachem needs killing, and you need to see which side you should believe in. I'll be back shortly. In the meantime, dig up Beachem's paper and start working on getting my bounty money.

CHAPTER 25

Justice walked down the dusty street, pushed through the batwing doors, and stepped into the gloomy, mostly empty confines of The Cistern.

He scanned the room ready for action.

At one of the back tables, a bushy black beard pointed toward the ceiling as its owner drained a mug of beer.

The man slammed the empty mug angrily onto the table. "Barkeep!"

The bartender, however, was staring wide-eyed at Justice, as were the saloon's few remaining customers.

The piano went silent, and people started scrambling to get out of the way.

It would've been an easy thing to drill Beachem right then and there, but Justice waited, and a second later the outlaw spotted him.

A sneering grin split his black beard, and he shot to his feet, hands flexed at his sides. "You."

Unlike Johnson, Beachem didn't seem frightened to recognize Justice. He sounded amused.

"Yes, me. And now, us. We got unfinished business."

A MAN CALLED JUSTICE

Beachem rocked from side to side twitching with eagerness. "I already killed you once. I'll kill you again. You hear that everyone? I'm gonna kill this man! Y'all are about to see who's the quickest draw in the territory. Harvey Beachem, that's who."

"You gonna draw, or are you fixing to talk me to death, Beachem?"

Beachem shouted wordlessly and grabbed his pistol.

He was fast.

Justice had to give the twitchy outlaw that much credit.

But not fast enough.

Just as Beachem's pistol cleared its holster, Justice nailed him in the belly. The bullet must have clipped Beachem's spine because he dropped like his legs had turned to water.

Beachem's pistol discharged wildly, then hit the floor and spun a few feet away. Growling, the outlaw humped awkwardly across the floor, reaching for his fallen weapon.

"Don't," Justice said, taking time now to aim his Colt more precisely.

Beachem cursed him and grabbed the wayward pistol.

Justice shot him in the shoulder.

Beachem cried out, released the pistol, and fell back. His right arm lay like a dead thing at his side. His left clutched at his belly wound.

"Shoulda killed you better... the first time," Beachem groaned. "Now... you done killed me."

"You're reaping what you sowed," Justice said. "You'd best start praying for forgiveness."

Beachem shook his head. "Don't deserve it, don't want it. Was always the fastest. But you... you done killed me. Tucker got a... telegram. Sent... four of us after you. Said you was special... one of them... silent justices. But I never... believed in such... claptrap."

One final twitch wracked Beachem, and then he eased back into death, still at last.

Three down, one to go.

After checking the bar for threats and finding none, Justice secured Beachem's weapon, a .45 Peacemaker with the trigger guard cut off. He searched his pockets and found poker chips, a pocketknife, a crumpled photo of an ugly woman with dark hair, three double-eagle twenty-dollar gold pieces, and a money belt packed with over three hundred dollars' worth of greenbacks.

Apparently, there was good money in being an outlaw... until you got killed, that was.

The saloon had emptied out. The barkeep peeked over the bar like a frightened prairie dog. "Is it over?"

"Beachem's over, that's for sure. But no, it ain't over yet. I got one more of them put in the ground. Man by the name of Del Mundo. And you can tell it far and wide that that's what I'm fixing to do."

A crowd had formed outside the bar. People held the batwings ajar, peeking into The Cistern with morbid interest.

Justice strode through the doors. Folks parted before him, giving him room, as if his very touch might confer death.

Perkins came stumping down the street, pale faced, gripping a shotgun across his body. Seeing Justice his mouth dropped open. "You outdrew Beachem?"

Justice nodded walking past the sheriff. "What's the bounty?"

Perkins followed, looking stunned. "Eleven hundred dollars. He was wanted for multiple murders and a whole string of other crimes."

"Well, he's not wanted anymore. He's dead." Justice started unhitching Beachem's Morgan from in front of the sheriff's office. "I just opened an account across the street. You can deposit my money there."

"Okay, Mr. Justice. Might take a couple of days but will do."

Justice turned to regard the sheriff and saw that he was smiling.

Which meant he'd rather deal with Justice than Beachem. No surprise there. But the trouble with cowardly men was they always focused on whatever was right in front of them. They lived in the moment, lacking character, and were always vulnerable to the next threat.

Question was did Perkins have any true character in him? Did he have the heart to change?

"You think on what I said, Perkins. It's high time to choose sides. You got two choices. Either ride with us or stand against us."

Perkins lifted his chin a little. "I'll ride with you boys. Make this official."

Justice clapped the man on the shoulder. "That's good. We just want to do what's right. It'll take a few days to get these ranchers together, and besides, I want to give the holdouts a little more time to come to their senses. I'll be in touch. Stay ready."

"I will, Mr. Justice. By gum, I will." Perkins was smiling now like a man surprised by a new dawn.

"That's good," Justice said, starting down the street with the Morgan. "In the meantime, you might want to let the undertaker know he's got a job down at The Cistern."

CHAPTER 26

Hector woke Justice a little past midnight.

"All quiet?" Justice asked.

"Except for some wolves in the distance, yes."

"We're talking the four-legged variety, right?"

"Yes, the better and less dangerous variety of the two. Do you think Tucker will be afraid now that you've killed Beachem?"

"Can't rightly say. It should call his bluff, anyway. Maybe when the association rides out there we'll find he's packed his bags and fled the territory. But I kindly doubt it."

"Yeah. That Morgan is a nice horse. I'm glad we will soon finish the new stable. You will be gone how many days?"

"Two nights, I reckon, three at the most."

"We will finish before you return."

"That's great news. And in the meantime, you and Jorge feel free to sleep in the ranch house while we're away. I know Nora won't mind you spreading your bed rolls in there, and it should be more comfortable than the barn."

"We don't mind the barn. But thank you. Perhaps we will."

"Make yourselves at home. Use whatever food you want.

I'll replace it when we get back. There's a deck of cards next to the sugar bowl. And if Tucker's men do raid the ranch while we're away, remember what I said."

"Don't get into a fight if we can avoid it."

"That's right. Horses and cattle we can replace."

Hector nodded, and the two men went their separate ways; Justice heading outside with the Winchester, Hector bedding down beside his son, who snored softly with the deep slumber of a young man after a long day's work.

As Justice emerged from the barn a shadow rose and trotted over, his constant companion, Rafer, ready to stand watch beside him.

Justice went to the small fire Hector had been tending, poured himself a cup of coffee, and moved back into the darkness, not wanting to spoil his night vision.

The moon was nearly full, and he could see a good distance out across the land.

In the foothills to the north wolves started howling again.

Rafer turned in that direction, tail held high like a bushy battle standard. The half-wild dog huffed once then fell silent.

Justice figured the dog had plenty of wolf blood coursing through that lean, shaggy body. Hearing his wild cousins must stir something in his bone marrow.

Justice's thoughts returned again to Beachem's dying words.

What was a silent justice? The term meant nothing to him, though it did jar him on a gut level.

It sounded like some kind of lawman. Unconsciously, he raised a hand to his chest and brushed his fingertips over the silver star that had become part of him.

The only word still recognizable on its largely melted surface—*Justice*—seemed to corroborate Beachem's story.

He racked his brain. Did any lawman's badge read *Justice?*

None that he knew of. He supposed it could have been designed by some small town, folks hiring him to uphold the law and engraving whatever they saw fit on a silver badge.

But Beachem had made it sound like a special lawman.

No matter the meaning it was an odd name. The *justice* part wasn't hard to figure. It almost certainly referred to some kind of lawman. But why *silent?*

Whatever the case, this strange little phrase was his first big step toward tracking down his past.

Maybe someone in Santa Fe would know something.

He looked forward to the trip and believed everything was in order.

After leaving Perkins to deal with Beachem, he'd acted on behalf of Nora and sent off a telegram to her sister letting Mary know Nora and Eli would be visiting the next day. It wasn't much notice, but it was better than showing up out of the blue. He paid an extra dollar to have the message delivered rapidly in person.

He'd gotten a big surprise at the livery when he finally got around to checking Beachem's saddle bags.

Only a brazen outlaw with the outsized confidence of Beachem would be so bold as to leave the Morgan tethered and unattended with the Sharps carbine in the boot and what he'd been hiding in his bags.

At first glance, Justice discovered what he would have expected: ammunition; half a bottle of whiskey; a Webley Bulldog; a stained and battered deck of cards; and another picture of the ugly, dark-haired woman, this one unfortunately displaying the unsmiling woman with most of her clothes missing.

Beneath the ammunition Justice discovered a false bottom in one bag. Pulling it aside he found a dozen bars of gold, each with a five-ounce mark stamped at its center.

That was a lot of money.

He went back into the bank and introduced himself to the manager, Percy Littlefield, explaining that Sheriff Perkins should soon be making a deposit in his account and asking Littlefield to take a look at the gold he'd found in Beachem's saddlebag.

Littlefield offered the standard 20 dollars per ounce for the gold, asking only a one-percent transaction fee.

Justice accepted and deposited most of it in his and Nora's joint account.

At home Nora saw the strange horse and, remembering Justice's description of Beachem's Morgan, came running out, checking him for injuries and asking what had happened.

Once he'd finished telling her, Nora surprised him by hugging him in front of Hector and Jorge, who had come out to see what was going on.

She surprised him again by weeping tears of relief and joy.

"Praise God," Nora said, clasping her hands together and turning her blue eyes skyward. "Thank you, Lord, for delivering Justice safely home to us."

And then Nora had surprised him a third time, adding, "And thank you, Lord, for bringing down your vengeance upon that wicked man!"

When Eli figured out what had happened, he hooted with excitement and gunned down a dozen Beachems with a Colt formed by the thumb and pointer finger of his left hand.

Later, after supper, with the boy in bed and Hector and Jorge playing cards outside, Justice and Nora had a chance to talk more.

She was excited for the trip to Santa Fe. Not just to see her family, she explained, but also to get away, especially after what had happened with Beachem.

"It'll all be over soon," he told her. "When we get back, Diego and the other ranchers will be ready to ride."

"And then?"

"I still have to track down Del Mundo."

Nora shuddered but did not try to dissuade him. She cared deeply about Justice but also understood he was a man of his word and was determined to avenge himself on Del Mundo. Besides, she was a pragmatic woman and understood that so long as Del Mundo remained alive, they would always be looking over their shoulders. She had total faith in Justice.

But another worry nagged her.

"What about after that?" she asked.

"I don't know. I'm going to ask around Santa Fe and see if anybody recognizes me or can tell me anything else about that phrase Beachem used, *silent justice.*"

"And if you do learn something…"

"I'll have to follow any leads. I need to know who I am, Nora. I need to make sure I don't have people out there counting on me. I couldn't bear the thought of neglecting folks like you and Eli, of letting them suffer somewhere out there in the world, waiting on me, wondering why I hadn't come back to them."

"If you leave Eli and I will suffer plenty."

"So will I, Nora. So will I."

"I'm sorry. It isn't fair of me to say these things. I know you're doing the decent thing, the right thing. I'm just being selfish is all."

"You're being sensible. I love my life here with you and Eli. I wouldn't want to trade it for anything in the world. But I have to know the truth. Know this, though. No matter what happens, I will not forget you."

"We won't forget you either, Justice. Not ever. That is a promise."

"When I was in town I opened an account with both our names on it."

"You put my name on your account?"

"Our account, not mine. Beachem was carting some gold in his saddlebags. I sold it and deposited seven hundred dollars. Once the bounty gets deposited, we'll have eighteen hundred dollars in there."

"Eighteen hundred dollars? It doesn't seem possible."

"Well, it is possible. It's more than possible. It's real. Now, I'm guessing that kind of money will ease your mind a touch."

"You have a gift for understatement, Justice. That kind of money is a Godsend. It wipes out all my worries… at least all of the worries that can be fixed with money. But I still don't understand. I have no right to your money, Justice."

"My money is your money, Nora. I wouldn't even be alive if it weren't for you."

"And without you, I would've been used by Tate and likely be dead or run off the ranch by now. As I've said all along, there is no debt."

"Not to you. But to me. And my debt to you transcends money. I will always be grateful and do my best to help you."

"And see me?"

"I hope so, Nora."

"I hope so, too, Justice. I hope so with all my heart and soul."

CHAPTER 27

The next morning Justice woke early, shaved, and put on a clean shirt for the stagecoach trip. It would be good, given the coming storm with Tucker, to know that Nora and Eli would be safe with her sister in Santa Fe for a couple of weeks.

He got the mules hitched and the wagon ready.

A short time later Nora came out of the house looking very pretty in a flower-print dress she had made for the occasion. The style and cut were modest enough, but the tailored dress nonetheless drew Justice's eyes.

Nora was a well-formed woman, that was for sure.

Opening his money belt, he handed her $100.

She looked at the fistful of greenbacks like he'd handed her a stick of sparking dynamite. "That's a lot of money."

"It is."

"Well, what's it for?"

"Whatever you need. And there should be enough there for anything you want, too. I don't want you and Eli pinching pennies in Santa Fe. Have a good time. They'll have bigger mercantiles there. Pick up whatever you want. Clothing, whatever, even if you need to buy new suitcases to cart it all home."

"Oh Justice, you are going to spoil me."

"I aim to. If there's a woman who deserves spoiling, it's you."

"I feel the same way about you. I just wish—"

She trailed off, but they both knew what she meant. Knew it and felt it.

They rode into Dos Pesos early, left the wagon and mules with Manuel at the livery, and headed to the Dos Pesos Inn, where Justice treated them to a hearty breakfast to hold them over during the first leg of the long stagecoach trip.

Justice loaded up, ordering eggs and bacon and fried potatoes with diced onion and pepper, which he slathered in hot sauce.

Nora ignored her food for a moment, studying the newspaper instead.

BADMAN BEACHEM GUNNED DOWN IN DOS PESOS SALOON!

Her eyes flicked back and forth reading the article.

Eli watched her with great interest. "What's it say, Mama?"

Nora suppressed a small smile. "It explains how Justice saved this town from a very bad man, Eli. This Harvey Beachem was wanted for a whole slew of crimes, including murder."

The boy grinned at Justice. "But you murdered him, huh, Justice?"

Justice frowned thoughtfully and laid a hand on the exuberant boy's arm. "No, son. I did not murder him. I killed him in a fair fight, but I did not murder him."

"What's the difference?"

"Well, it's complicated and involves certain legalities, but at the heart of the matter it's as simple as the difference

JOHN DEACON

between good and evil. Sometimes a good man must kill to protect himself and others. A bad man kills for fun or profit."

Eli nodded, a bit sobered but still proud to be sharing the table with a good man who'd killed a bad man.

"Murderers like Beachem are pure evil, Eli," Nora said. "Sadly, they force good men like Justice into killing them."

"Well, I'm glad he's dead," Eli pronounced.

"So am I," Justice said. "Now, Mrs. Eckert, if you'll let me see that paper, please, I'm hoping to find something that interests me much more than a recounting of yesterday's unpleasantness in The Cistern."

She handed him the *Dos Pesos Gazette*.

He turned the page, and a huge smile spread across his face.

"What is it?" Nora asked.

He turned the paper so she could see the full-page ad.

"It's official. The River Valley Cattleman's Association has announced itself. Between this proclamation, our courthouse business, and Sheriff Perkins riding along, our position is impeccable. If Tucker tries to fight us it's going to look very bad on him."

"Will he care?"

"I think so. There are many types of bad men. You take your Tates and Beachems, they're like wild animals, sniffing around, living in the moment. They're mean and nasty, low down and dangerous. They don't spend much time thinking ahead, and even if they set a goal, they don't have the backbone or character to actually work toward it."

He took a sip of coffee and continued. "But you take a man like Tucker, he's ambitious. He dreams big and is willing to do whatever it takes to see those dreams come to fruition. He understands men like Tate and Beachem and uses them to get what he wants, which is more than a pile of money or a stretch of good land. Tucker wants respect and power.

"He doesn't just want land. He wants to rule the land. But to achieve that he has to mind the impression he makes with the general public. Sure, he can step on some toes along the way. Out here in the West it's almost expected of so-called great men. But he doesn't want the whole territory knowing he's a scoundrel, or it won't matter how much land, cattle, or money he's got. He'll never be able to use his wealth to leverage the type of social power he desires."

"So, it's over then?" Nora said with a hopeful smile.

Justice shook his head. "No ma'am, I don't reckon it is. But these moves I've mentioned, they're gonna make Tucker stop and think, that's for sure, and after we make a united show of force, it might really be over."

At nine they boarded the stagecoach, which was driven by a Mr. A.W. Mosely. Riding next to him was Carlton Traits, a hard-looking older man clutching a coach gun.

Within the carriage they met two passengers who had boarded earlier. A beefy feed salesman named Preston and a bright-faced young woman named Lily Driscoll, who, after three months at her grandparents' ranch down on the Llano Estacado, was excited to be making the trip home to Santa Fe, what she now regarded as the absolute model of civilized society.

Preston nodded off, but Lily turned out to be quite the talker.

They made a few stops along the way, picking up four more passengers, including, unfortunately, a filthy man who smelled like he hadn't bathed in a month. The only saving grace was that the stench of the man seemed to rein in the chatter of Lily, who leaned away from the man, looking ill.

The ride was long and bumpy, but it wasn't too bad. Bandits were a real threat along the coach roads of New Mexico Territory, but luckily, they had no such trouble this day. They broke for a lunch of beans and rice at a way station, swapped out horses, then got back on the trail and arrived in Santa Fe early that evening.

They did not go straight to Mary's house. It was late for that, and though neither Justice nor Nora said so aloud, they wanted to spend more time together before parting. So they booked rooms at a nice hotel and had a lovely dinner together.

They all got the special, buffalo steak with fried potatoes and onions and grilled tomato slices on the side. Nora ordered a glass of wine, Justice enjoyed a couple of beers, and Eli gleefully sucked down a sarsaparilla.

Justice savored his beers just watching his companions. How he loved watching them simply eat and drink and converse.

It was still light out when they finished, so Justice paid and left a good tip and escorted Nora and Eli on an evening walk. It was pleasant and, as the sun settled in the western horizon, breathtakingly beautiful.

But not as beautiful as Nora when the splintering daylight cast her lovely features in roseate hues. Again, Justice reined in his powerful desire. Oh, how he loved this woman—loved her and desired her.

He could tell by her smile that she detected his warmth and desire and reciprocated on both counts. The connection between them couldn't be stronger, it seemed; and yet it somehow managed to grow stronger with each passing day as they lived and worked and talked together.

"I just realized something," Nora said.

"What's that?"

She gave an embarrassed laugh. "Never mind. It's such an obvious thought, you'll think me foolish for even mentioning it."

"Don't do that, Nora. I always want to hear what's on

your mind, no matter how trivial, and I would never think you foolish."

"Well, I just realized that tomorrow, when you drop us off at Mary's, it'll be the first time since meeting you that we will be apart."

He nodded. "I'm not looking forward to that."

"I wish you were coming with us."

"Yeah, Justice!" Eli piped up. "Please come with us!"

"I am."

Nora gave a playful frown. "*Staying* with us, I mean, not turning around and heading straight back to the ranch."

"Another time, perhaps. But the cattleman's association is planning on visiting Tucker in three days, and they're counting on me to ride with them."

Nora shook her head and sighed heavily. "If it weren't for men like Tucker…"

"If it weren't for men like Tucker, you and I never even would've met."

"I suppose you're right."

Justice grinned. "Once in a while, anyway."

Nora brushed her fingertips over his arm, and Justice reckoned she was struggling against her own desires, too. "I still wish you were coming with us."

"You'll be all right. You got your pocket pistol, right?" He'd given her the derringer he'd taken off Johnson and made her promise to carry it always.

"Yes sir. I won't go anywhere without it. But I don't just want you along for protection."

"I understand."

"I'm going to miss you."

"Me, too!" Eli said.

"And I'll miss you two twice as bad. Hey, at least y'all have each other. Besides, I have a feeling you're gonna be too busy to think of me, Nora, what with the baby coming and all the catching up with family you'll have to do."

He crouched down putting his hands on Eli's shoulders and looked the boy in the eyes. They were the spitting image of Nora's eyes, and Justice's heart swelled with love for this child. "And you are gonna be so busy seeing new things and playing with your cousins that you won't have time to think of old Justice."

"Yes, I will!" Eli said. "And I'll pray for you every night."

"Well, I certainly do appreciate that, son."

"And if you think anything would make me too busy to think of you," Nora said, mock-crossly, "you don't know me half so well as I thought you did, Mr. Justice."

CHAPTER 28

Tucker was furious. Del Mundo was frightened. Haversham was amused.

It was going to be interesting, the lawyer thought as he polished the lenses of his spectacles, to see how Tucker and Del Mundo weathered this storm.

Especially because Haversham was about to magnify its ferocity.

"Just how did they make this happen so quickly?" Tucker demanded, jabbing a fat finger at the newspaper, which lay open to the full-page spread announcing the creation, sanctification, and purpose of the River Valley Cattleman's Association. He turned toward Haversham. "You know the law. Is this even legal?"

Haversham returned his glasses to his nose and saw that Tucker's beefy face had gone a dangerous shade of red.

"It certainly appears legal, Mr. Tucker. Setting up an organization like this is actually quite simple, especially in a territory like this, where the government wants all the help it can get to establish law and order. The real trouble with putting together an association of ranchers isn't the legal hurdles one must clear to make it official; the real trouble is the ranchers themselves. Generally speaking, these small rancher types, especially on a frontier like this, would rather die alone than join together in any official or binding way."

Tucker pounded a big fist down on his ridiculously huge desk. "That's exactly what I mean! How could they come together so quickly?"

"There is only one possible explanation," Haversham said with a smile. "Mr. Justice."

"Mr. Justice. What a stupid name! Who is this man, anyway?"

Haversham spread his soft hands. "Whoever he is, I would bet my bottom dollar that he was the driving force behind this cattleman's association. For as fiercely independent as these small ranchers are, they are not necessarily stupid, and they do respect one thing: strength. If Mr. Justice has displayed one attribute, it is strength. Wouldn't you agree, Mr. Del Mundo?"

"Huh?" the hulking redhead grunted, snapping out of his daze. He had been staring dumbfounded at the newspaper, not at the announcement that had so enraged Mr. Tucker but at the facing page, his eyes going out of focus as if trying to stare through the print to the opposite side, the paper's front page, which stated in all caps, *BADMAN BEACHEM GUNNED DOWN IN DOS PESOS SALOON!*

Tucker paced back and forth behind his colossal desk. "The boss told me these ranchers would never come together the way they did back in—"

"Surely, you aren't questioning our employer, are you?" Haversham said, sitting up a bit straighter, his interest sharpening even further. "Would you like me to send him a telegram expressing your displeasure?"

That took the bluster out of Tucker. "No. Of course not. I'm not questioning him. I'm just saying—"

"Or perhaps you've come to realize you do require the services of Mr. Rose after all?"

Tucker pounded his desk again, hammering it with all the tremendous force of a big man accustomed to getting his way through brute strength. "No! We do not need Rose. We will handle this ourselves. Del Mundo, how come you haven't killed this so-called Mr. Justice?"

"That's the thing, boss," Del Mundo said. Suddenly, all the color had drained from the face of this muscular savage, who never hesitated to commit the most heinous acts. "We did kill him."

"He seems to be getting around pretty well for a dead man."

Del Mundo stared glassily down at the paper. "His heart stopped."

"Apparently, it started up again, unless you're telling me he's a ghost. Is that what you're saying, Del Mundo? That a ghost gunned down your cronies?"

"He was dead. That's all I'm saying, Mr. Tucker."

"Well, now he needs killing all over again. And this time, Del Mundo, do a better job of it. Make sure he stays dead."

Del Mundo regarded Tucker with bulging eyes and licked his lips.

The brute's terror was delicious to Haversham, who said, "Did you not hear Mr. Tucker?"

"I heard him, all right. But see, the trouble is, I can't kill him."

"Why in the world not?" Tucker bellowed. "That's your job, isn't it? I have a problem, you fix it. And this Mr. Justice is a certified problem if ever there was one. Now, you go out tonight and don't come back till he's dead. If Mr. Haversham is right, he's the force holding together all these ranchers. You kill him, they'll go back to their solitary ways."

"You are likely correct, sir," Haversham said.

"Well, Del Mundo, what are waiting for? Go kill him!"

Del Mundo looked back and forth between them, wringing his hat like it was the neck of a woman no longer of use to him. "I can't kill him, boss. He just comes and goes like a ghost. I asked around. Nobody knows where he lives."

Oh yes, it was glorious, Haversham thought, watching this primitive killer writhe in horror. Not on moral grounds, of course—Haversham felt nothing for the many victims of Del Mundo—but because the situation was so perfectly ironic, the fearless marauder ready to run for his life.

Would Del Mundo run for his life? They were about to find out.

Because now, at last, Haversham was about to play the card he'd been hiding up his sleeve. The card that would likely unman Del Mundo and give Tucker everything he needed to handle this situation in his ham-fisted way, putting him to the test and clarifying Haversham's own position and the likely paths he would need to travel to return once more to wealth, civilization, and the finer things in life.

He could all but taste the renowned seafood of San Francisco's restaurants, all but hear the clink of silver on good China, all but smell the delicate floral perfume of powdered ladies, all but feel their lace and soft flesh as he groped them beneath the table.

Haversham smiled. "I know where Justice lives."

CHAPTER 29

The next morning they caught a carriage and crossed into Santa Fe. It was a big, bustling town, and Justice knew at once that he had visited at some point during his prior existence.

Was this his hometown?

He didn't think so, but he found as they headed for her sister's home that the streets were indeed familiar, and he suspected he had visited more than once, perhaps even many times.

Gnarled oak trees shaded Mary's neat little adobe house. A low whitewashed wall enclosed the lot, which Justice estimated to be an acre or so. Between the house and stable he saw a vegetable garden and the strutting white forms of chickens on their never-ending quest for forage.

Then a passel of women and children came pouring out of the house, all of them smiling and calling Nora and Eli's names.

Justice paused by the front gate smiling and watched as Nora and Eli rushed forward and were swallowed up by this wave of loving humanity.

He lingered long enough to meet folks, including Nora's mother, a handsome woman who studied him with a wise smile and, he thought, approving eyes; a very pregnant Mary, who wept for joy to be reunited with Nora and Eli; and three of Nora's teenaged sisters, who made no secret of their approval of Nora's "gentleman friend."

The numerous children barely noticed him, of course. After marveling briefly over his height, they whirled around Eli, some of them meeting him for the first time, others half-remembering him, in the manner of playful wolf pups welcoming another into the pack. Seconds later they ran off together toward whatever wonderful adventures awaited them.

The women invited Justice inside, but he begged off, explaining that he had business to see to here in Santa Fe before heading back to the ranch.

He and Nora smiled at each other, eyes locked together, and said a restrained goodbye. He reminded her to send word when she was ready for him to come back and fetch them, and she said she would.

"Just spend the extra money and have a messenger ride out to the ranch," he told her. Then he tipped his hat and returned to the waiting coach.

"Take me to the sheriff's office."

As the coach pulled away from the curb, Justice looked back toward the quaint little house and saw Nora hesitate in the doorway, watching him go.

He waved.

Nora raised a hand to her lips and blew him a secret kiss, and he was all smiles as the coach turned the corner and headed back into the heart of Santa Fe.

Ten minutes later he paid the coachman and entered the Santa Fe Sheriff's Office, where he introduced himself to the two men inside.

One was young and lean and clean shaven with the bright eyes of a man who lived a clean life and very much believed in the work of his days.

The other man was fortyish, slim, and serious with short, dark hair; a neatly trimmed mustache; and dark, close-set eyes that clearly brooked no nonsense. He dressed not in Western fashion but in a dark suit, looking like he'd just arrived from some Eastern metropolis.

"I'm Sheriff J.T. Huff, and this is my deputy, Thomas Peele. What can we do for you, Mr. Justice?"

"Well, I reckon you've already answered my first question. You men don't know me, do you?"

Sheriff Huff looked at him strangely. "No, I don't believe so."

"I never seen you before, Mister," Deputy Peele chimed in.

Justice explained his situation, starting with waking in Nora's ranch house and wrapping up with his trip here. He included a bit of the conflict awaiting him at the ranch but didn't focus on it. He was here to investigate his past, not his present.

"That is quite a story, Mr. Justice," Sheriff Huff said. "I do wish I could help you, but I don't know what to say."

"Could we see the badge?" Peele asked.

Justice unbuttoned his shirt and showed them the silver star embedded in his chest.

"That must've smarted!" the amazed deputy said. "I've never seen such a thing."

By the look on Huff's face, however, Justice reckoned maybe he had.

The sheriff studied the badge, then regarded Justice seriously, almost warily. "That badge reads *Justice*. Any idea where it comes from? What organization, I mean?"

"No sir, but one of the outlaws I recently dispatched, a man by the name of Harvey Beachem, said something."

Peele's eyes bulged. "You bagged Beachem? He's a bad man—and fast as a rattler, I hear."

"He was. Now, he's just dead. Anyway, Beachem said I was supposed to be some kind of lawman called a silent justice."

Now, Huff's eyes swelled, too.

"A silent justice, you say?"

"Yes sir. Beachem said his boss, Tucker, got word of a silent justice and sent these four men after me."

"Only four? If you're a silent justice, they're lucky you didn't kill them all."

Justice shrugged. He had no memory of how, precisely, they had taken him. "I surely would appreciate anything you could tell me about silent justices."

"I don't know much, just stories I've heard here and there over the years... and not often. To tell you the truth I never believed the stories. They sounded like tall tales. Would you indulge me a short experiment, Mr. Justice?"

"Sure, if it'll help me get answers."

"I want to see how fast you can draw that pistol."

CHAPTER 30

J ustice angled himself away from the men and drew his
Colt. He put some speed on it. Some but not all. A man
should never reveal just how dangerous he is, even to
friends, until it is absolutely necessary.

Deputy Peele practically gasped. "Never saw nobody so
fast as that before."

"Neither have I," Huff agreed. "Are you accurate with that
thing?"

"Good enough to get the job done."

"Comfortable with a rifle?"

"Very."

"Shotguns, derringers, different sorts of pistols?"

"I reckon so. Weapons are natural to me."

"Can you operate a Gatlin gun?"

Justice thought for a second. "Yes."

"How about weapons other than firearms?"

"Such as?"

"Like that big Bowie you're wearing."

"I reckon so."

"Bows and arrows? Tomahawks?"

Justice shrugged. In his mind, however, he imagined firing a bow and arrow and everything seemed familiar. "I believe I am proficient with a bow. The other day I threw a tomahawk and nailed a target forty feet away, no problem."

"What about hand to hand?" Huff asked, retrieving a set of keys from his desk. The keyring ran through a six-inch length of wooden dowel. "Imagine this was a knife and I was looking to run you through. Easy now, I'm not looking to break any bones."

Justice shrugged and beckoned.

Huff came at him faster than he'd expected, swinging the makeshift knife full speed at his stomach.

Justice didn't even have to think about his defense. His body reacted, smoothly and naturally, as if it had in the past fended off dozens of blades.

Twisting aside he snatched Huff's wrist and yanked, using the sheriff's own momentum to pull him off-balance. Justice's hip swiveled automatically, and his knee jammed just as automatically into Huff's midsection knocking the wind from his lungs.

Luckily, Justice had the wherewithal to pull the strike, or he might have done some serious damage. Not that this damage would've much factored into things if Huff had been a real assailant with a real knife, because a second after Justice landed the kick, he'd jerked Huff's own hand back toward him and rapped the point of the dowel against the sheriff's side and abdomen several times.

Peele laughed with amazement.

Even Huff cracked a slight smile as he rubbed his stomach. "Well, I'll be darned. You just killed me, Mr. Justice. Could the tales really be true?"

"I don't mean to be pushy, Sheriff Huff, but I remain in the dark over here."

"The way I hear it—and again, I never put any stock in these stories; in my mind they were just that, stories, told by lawmen and outlaws, over campfires and whiskey—but the way I heard it, there are a small number of men—some say three, some say seven—appointed to roam the country of their own accord, setting things straight."

"Like vigilantes?"

"Sort of, I guess. They do take the law into their own hands, but like I said, they are appointed."

"Appointed by who?"

Huff shrugged. "I've heard stories. Some say the president himself. Whatever the case, these silent justices are supposed to be men of impeccable skill and character. They are the toughest of the tough, the bravest of the brave, and totally incorruptible. Also, they are trained to master all conceivable weapons, including their own bodies."

"Toward what end?"

"Justice," Huff said. "They go where they want and do as they please but keep things quiet."

"Silent," Peele said, eyes gleaming. "This is amazing!"

"It's hearsay, is what it is," Huff said, "and all of this stays here in this office, you understand me, Deputy Peele?"

"Yes sir."

"I reckon if it got out that our friend here might be a silent justice, bad men from all over the West would be lining up to try him. It boggles the mind, but there is never a shortage of men willing to die with a bullet in their belly."

"Or a knife in their side," Peele said. "I've never seen anything like that."

"What else can you tell me about these silent justices?" Justice asked.

"Unfortunately, not much. I've never talked to anyone who even claimed to have met one in person. Like I said, these are campfire tales best told after the whiskey starts flowing. Outlaws never open their mouths without lying, and most lawmen, when drinking with friends, aren't much better. So I never really put much stock in the stories, but I must say you have made me reconsider my position... dramatically."

"Well, I appreciate your time," Justice said, figuring he'd better get on with his day. He found himself believing Huff's suspicions, not that this information did him much good. At least it seemed to confirm Beachem's dying words. Perhaps by asking others about the silent justices, he would find his way back.

"It is a pleasure to meet you, Mr. Justice," Huff said, shaking his hand again. "You are a man I hope to always have on my side."

"Count on it. If you remember anything else about these silent justices, do me a favor and send me a telegram in Dos Pesos, all right?"

"I absolutely will," Huff said. "In the meantime, I will contact some friends and see if they can provide any additional information. Before you leave jot down where you're staying. I'll be in touch no matter what I hear, even if it's just crickets. And best of luck to you. If you think of it, I'd appreciate receiving word of how things go for you."

"Will do."

"Now," Sheriff Huff said, "is there anything we can help you with here in Santa Fe?"

"I figured in a town this size I might be able to buy a top horse. Could you direct me to Santa Fe's best livery?"

"Sure. The man to see is Luke Martinez. His place is only a few blocks from here. Take a left out our door then take another left onto your first cross street. The livery's two blocks further on. You can't miss it."

"Thank you."

"Anything else we can do for you?"

"Yeah, I reckon there maybe is one more thing I'd like to get my hands on, but I reckon it might be difficult to procure without your assistance. I doubt I'll even end up needing it, but if I do, there is no substitute."

CHAPTER 31

J ustice found the livery with no trouble.

Luke Martinez was younger than Justice would have expected, a smiling man barely into his twenties, but the hostler had already built up quite a business and clearly knew his horses.

Justice already had a surplus of horses thanks to the outlaws he'd killed, but the more time he spent with himself the more he realized that he loved not only women, children, and weapons but also horses.

Visiting the best livery in Santa Fe presented a rare opportunity. He explained that he was interested in only the finest horse.

"You talking looks, performance, or both?" Martinez asked.

"Performance. I don't care what the horse looks like so long as it's fast, responds well, and has plenty of endurance.

"I should have something to fit your needs," Martinez said. "I have good stock at the moment."

He wasn't kidding.

Martinez led Justice to a corral where several beautiful horses awaited.

Justice considered all of the animals but truly had eyes for only one.

"Let's talk about that steel dust over yonder."

"I see you got an eye for horseflesh, Mr. Justice. That's the finest horse I got. Five-year-old stallion. Fast and strong and smart as a whip."

They walked over.

"He can be a bit standoffish is all," Martinez said as Justice lifted a hand.

Justice grinned at that. Standoffish. Stallions were a touch more than standoffish. But it was all part of the game, and he was confident he could handle this magnificent horse.

Surprisingly, the stallion didn't flinch as Justice's hand smoothed over his soft, warm nose.

"How much you want for him?"

"That horse? Like I said, he's my best. I couldn't let him go for less than five hundred dollars."

Justice chuckled. "That's too much, even for a horse this fine."

Martinez smiled, feigning incredulity. "Too much? You lack vision, Mr. Justice. If you have the *cojones* to race this horse, you will earn your money back before the first snow falls this year."

Justice shook his head. "Sheriff Huff said you had the best horses. He neglected to inform me that you were a high-wayman to boot. I'll give you two fifty."

"Two hundred and fifty? You would have to change your name to Mr. Injustice if I gave you this horse for a penny less than four hundred."

They went back and forth, enjoying the haggling, and finally settled on a price of three hundred and seventy-five dollars with Martinez agreeing to throw in a saddle, bags, and all the tack Justice needed to ride this horse home, along with a sack of oats.

They shook hands, both of them pleased with the transaction.

"Get everything ready," Justice told him, slinging the saddlebags over one shoulder, "and I'll be back after I run a few errands."

He walked off and procured the other thing he needed, thanks to a note from Sheriff Huff, then continued to a large dry goods store, where he bought matches, ammo, a canteen, a bedroll, a slicker he could use to keep the dew off him, rope, some jerky, crackers, and several cans of peaches. He picked up a little bottle of perfume for Nora and bought a McGuffey primer and a fistful of hard candy for Eli.

Though he was wearing his Colt, he bought another Winchester and plenty of ammo. He didn't expect trouble, but better safe than sorry. New Mexico Territory was still rife with bad men, and there was no surer way to bring them down on yourself than to travel with an empty rifle boot.

He stopped at a busy cafe and enjoyed an early dinner of *carne adovada* with fresh corn tortillas, cilantro, and diced onions. He washed that down with a cold *cerveza*, then ambled over to the livery and got his new steel dust.

He was more than satisfied with the purchase. Yes, he had paid a lot of money for the stallion, double what a man might expect to pay for a top saddle horse, but he still felt like he'd done well. This was a magnificent animal, and he couldn't wait to get him onto the trail.

Leaving town he whispered to the steel dust, who gave him no trouble. "What am I gonna call you, huh? A horse as fine as you needs a good name."

He studied the horse for a moment, rubbing the stallion's muscular neck and seeing real intelligence in his big, dark eyes.

"I got it. There's only one name for a steel dust whose strong, fast, streamlined, and sharp-witted. Your name is Dagger."

The horse did not object.

They hit the trail. He could make it back to Dos Pesos by midnight if he pushed it, but instead he took his time, appreciating his new horse and admiring the lofty, fir-bearded mountain peaks that dominated the northern horizon.

With each passing mile Justice became more convinced that he'd come out on top with Martinez. Dagger was a fine horse, the sort of animal a man spends his whole life dreaming of owning.

He paused every couple of hours to water and rest the stallion, ground hitching him so he could forage.

During those quiet times Justice went back over everything that had happened and everything that he had learned, cherishing the sight of Nora blowing him a kiss; pondering what Sheriff Huff had related concerning silent justices; and anticipating how Tucker might react when the cattleman's association showed up at his front door.

Rather than pushing on through the night, Justice stopped short and bedded down off the beaten path and near the river, giving himself plenty of time to care for Dagger, whispering as he rubbed down and curried the magnificent creature and fed it some oats.

The night was warm, and he didn't bother with a fire, supping on jerky, crackers, and an airtight of peaches.

"You stand first watch, buddy," he told the steel dust and slipped into peaceful sleep.

CHAPTER 32

An hour before dusk Del Mundo got into position 400 yards from the ranch house. He lay prone upon the hard ground behind a screen of heavy scrub.

His horse was a quarter mile upriver, tethered within the cottonwoods where his crew waited for his gunshot.

Del Mundo wasn't fooling around. This matter ended tonight. He didn't just bring along three men, the way he had when Tucker told him to run off the Lopezes.

That crazy Lopez woman had shown him these ranchers weren't to be taken lightly.

That went double for this Mr. Justice.

More than double, in fact. That's why he'd brought along a dozen rifles to make sure they settled Justice's hash for good.

Though truth be told, it should take only one rifle to finish the job, Del Mundo's, so long as Justice cooperated and came out of the ranch house before dark.

The heavy Sharps rifle, its scope, and the tripod were all relics of Del Mundo's life prior to becoming a full-time outlaw.

Before the blowup in Hide Town that had put him on the run from the law, he'd been a buffalo hunter.

He'd ridden rough for a few years moving from place to place, throwing in with different gangs, taking what he needed or wanted by force. He even sidled into New Mexico Territory and rode with the Boys for a while before heading back to Texas.

He'd just been building his own gang when he'd run into Tucker in a Ft. Worth saloon.

The two men had connected instantly. They were both large men, men of action, men used to being in control of their lives and destinies.

Tucker was older and more legitimate in the eyes of the world, having run a big ranch with thousands of head, and the man had money. Big money. And he was throwing it around left and right, putting together a crew before pushing into the New Mexico Territory.

So Del Mundo had signed on. Half his gang drifted away. No surprise there. Most men you could count on to run a raid but not much beyond that.

Tate and Johnson stuck with him and shortly after crossing into the territory, they'd run into Harvey Beachem. Having worked with the twitchy gunslinger before, Del Mundo vouched for him, and Tucker brought him onto the payroll.

For months the four men had ruled this new land, going where they wanted and doing what they wanted.

Then Tucker had sent them after the lawman, calling him a silent justice.

Del Mundo had never heard the term. As a rule, he tried to avoid anyone or anything that had to do with the law, which seemed the best course of action to avoid having his neck stretched.

Beachem had shared stories over the campfire as they

rode out to intercept this lone lawman. Stories that Del Mundo had not believed at the time; stories of a silent justice gunning down three men all at the same time; stories of these silent justices operating in secret; each of them judge, jury, and executioner all rolled into one, taking out whole gangs singlehandedly.

You heard a lot of tall tales on the trail. And to Del Mundo this had sounded like one more whopper.

In fact, all that nonsense about the unkillable silent justices sounded like one of the biggest whoppers Del Mundo had ever heard.

Now Tate, Johnson, and Beachem were all dead.

They had killed this Mr. Justice, but somehow, he had managed to come back and kill all of them... except Del Mundo.

Which meant either the men had been mistaken about Justice's lack of a pulse or the man really had died then come back to life to have his revenge.

Del Mundo preferred the former idea, and when he spoke that was the one he mentioned.

But privately he suspected the latter to be true. The notion of this man returning from the grave to hunt them down one by one was kindly unnerving.

And in a testament to the absurdity of the human mind, Del Mundo, a veritable demon in human flesh, had over the course of the last several hours convinced himself that he was the victim of an attack by supernatural forces of darkness.

He was not a God-fearing man, let alone a God-loving man, but he feared whatever was happening here enough to etch a crude cross into the head of the big bullet that tipped the two-and-a-half-inch round now chambered in the Sharps.

If he'd had more time he would have ridden to the

church, taken some holy water, and forced the priest to put a spell on the bullet, too.

He was a man of the world and wanted nothing to do with God or religion or the forces of darkness, but the cross seemed like a good idea, and he hoped with its help to blow this boogeyman back into the netherworld so he could get on with life.

These were Del Mundo's thoughts as he hunkered down, waiting for Justice to show.

Given the dying light and the heavy scrub on this side, he could have gotten closer, probably even within two hundred yards, but why risk it?

He was a good shot with the Sharps, and even if he missed, a dozen men would go riding in there as soon as he pulled the trigger.

If Del Mundo or his men killed Justice, all would be well. Del Mundo would escape the forces of darkness, Tucker would have his valley, and it would be only a matter of time until Tucker rewarded Del Mundo with a big ranch of his own and enough money to live out the rest of his life in style.

On the other hand, if Del Mundo's crew went riding in there and this silent justice killed all twelve of them, Del Mundo would have time at this distance to hop on his horse and head for the hills.

If that happened, he wouldn't bother riding back to Tucker's. He'd just head out and start over someplace far away. Maybe up in Leadville or maybe backtrack to the Nations.

He could figure that out if it came to it. For now, he was counting on the Sharps, the cross-bearing .50 caliber bullet, and the twelve-gun raiding party to solve this problem.

The more he thought about it, the more confident he became. The mistake Tate, Johnson, and Beachem had made was getting close to Justice. He wouldn't make that same mistake.

The only trouble was the dimming light. What if Justice didn't step outside before darkness fell?

He chewed on that one for a moment and got his guts all twisted up.

Then he smiled.

His men were far enough back that they couldn't see a thing.

If Justice didn't come out Del Mundo would pull the trigger anyway.

Then they'd come whooping out of the cottonwoods and attack the ranch house.

Yes, he thought, proud of his cleverness. *This is why I'm the leader and they aren't. This is why I'm alive and Tate, Johnson, and Beachem are dead.*

Daylight faded.

Del Mundo panned back and forth with the scope, wishing Justice would just make his life easy and step outside. But he was running out of time.

He curled his finger over the trigger and was just about to pull it and summon his crew when, miracle of miracles, the ranch house door opened, and the man came striding out into the open.

CHAPTER 33

Hector Barrera came outside and called to the half-wild mutt, fixing to toss it some dinner scraps. After months on the trail it was nice cooking on a stove, sitting at a table, and knowing they'd be bedding down indoors.

Now, where was that dog?

It followed Justice everywhere, but as soon as he'd left, the beast had slunk off like a wolf into the scrub.

Hector had seen it a couple of times earlier in the day, lurking, watching, and waiting.

Some dogs were like that. Not mean, necessarily, but really cottoning to only one man.

"Hey dog," Hector called into the darkness and turned, looking for movement.

Then a mule kicked him in the back, and he fell the ground, his mouth full of dust and blood.

Blood?

He tried to get up, but his body wouldn't work right.

As he tried to wrap his head around what was happening, he registered the far-off rifle shot.

And as his body flooded with pain, he realized what had happened.

He hadn't been kicked by a mule. He'd been shot in the back.

He had to get back into the house, had to warn his son.

Pain rushed over him stealing his breath. He was hit hard and losing a lot of blood. His body jerked, and darkness squeezed his field of vision until it was like he was staring into a long tube.

He pointed this tube at the ranch house door and pushed through the pain and crawled toward his son. He tried to cry out, but he had no air, no voice.

He was dying. He knew that. He was hit hard and was dying, should already be dead, but love for his son powered him on, and he dragged across the short distance to the door and pounded on its lower edge.

He was vaguely aware of many hoofbeats and voices rushing toward him, men hooting and hollering out of the gathering darkness.

The door opened.

Jorge, who had been washing up and singing as he banged the pots and pans in the sink, hadn't heard the distant gunshot. Now, seeing his father, he suddenly looked not like the brave, durable man Hector was so proud of. He looked like the boy he had been all those years ago when his mother had died, and Hector and Jorge had struck out on their own, father and son, to make their lonely way in a world that offered few opportunities and no mercy.

"Papa!" Jorge shouted and hauled Hector inside.

Another bullet struck the door, blowing splinters into the air.

Jorge slammed it shut.

There was so much Hector wanted to tell his son. He wanted to tell him what had happened and what to do, wanted to tell him about the approaching riders, and most of all, wanted to tell him how proud he was of the man Jorge had become and how much he loved him; words he had never spoken and now, he realized too late, never would.

Hector died as the raiders reached the house.

———

RAFER LAY LOW GROWLING AS THE MEN ON HORSEBACK circled the house, firing their guns, shouting laughter as they shot out windows and blew holes through the walls and door.

For a time, one of the men inside fought with his rifle, shooting from one window then another.

Three of the raiders fell from their saddles.

Rafer wanted to rush from the scrub and tear out their throats, but his instincts told him to stay out of sight.

He did not understand the words the men shouted at the house but clearly understood the malice in their tone.

Three riders stopped shooting and came together. Suddenly, they were holding fire.

As the other men continued to shoot their guns, these three tossed their flaming torches through the open windows of the house.

Soon, flames engulfed the home, leaping high into the air, turning the night noon-day bright.

Into this circle of light rode yet another man, a large man with red hair who laughed louder than the rest.

The red-haired man dismounted and drew close to the flames, circling the inferno and occasionally firing his pistol, laughing all the while.

Rafer's hackles raised. It would be easy to rush forward and hamstring the red-haired man, to pull him down and tear out his laughing throat.

Rafer could all but taste the blood. But he remained motionless, biding his time with the terrible patience of ancient ancestors.

Justice would return, the dog thought as he watched the men take the horses and mules and set fire to the outbuildings.

Yes, everything here was gone, but Justice would return... and he would know what to do.

Rafer had more faith in Justice than he had in these other men, the living or the dead; more faith in Justice than anyone or anything else in his experience.

He would wait.

Justice would return.

And then things would be set right again.

Sometimes animals are smarter than men.

CHAPTER 34

J ustice broke camp early and saddled Dagger, marveling again over the stallion's size and fine lines.

What a beautiful animal.

He mounted up and took his time heading downriver, speaking softly to the horse as they traveled, drawing ever closer to Dos Pesos.

They paused twice along the way for rest and water and a bit of food—jerky and peaches for Justice and some riverside grazing for the horse—and they reached Dos Pesos at midday.

The day was hot and town was unusually quiet, almost eerily so.

Justice stopped at the mercantile and picked up a bottle of whiskey as thanks to Hector and Jorge, then went to the livery and paid Manuel Chavez, who was awestruck over Dagger.

He offered Justice three hundred for the horse. Then four. Then five.

Justice laughed, shaking his head. "Some things are not for sale, my friend. I'll be keeping him."

Dagger had held up well over the miles, but Justice was happy to give him a break as he climbed up into the wagon and headed home, trailing the beautiful horse behind with a long rope. He couldn't wait to see Hector and Jorge's reactions. They were men who appreciated good horseflesh, and Dagger was the best of the best.

Justice knew something was wrong when, drawing close, he realized the horizon was wrong.

Soon he detected pale smoke wafting up from the darkened ground where Nora's home and outbuildings should have been.

Laying the Winchester across his lap he snapped the reins, urging the mules toward the devastation.

He didn't waste any time wondering what had happened. He knew what had happened. Tucker's men, likely led by Del Mundo, had raided the ranch and burned it to the ground.

His only question now was for Hector and Jorge.

A moment later, he crossed the tracks of the raiders. Tucker had sent many horses.

Reaching the ranch he called out for Hector and Jorge.

They were gone. Everything was gone. The buildings, the animals, everything.

Then Rafer came trotting out of the scrub.

Good. At least they hadn't killed the dog.

Justice hopped down off the wagon. The mules fidgeted, uneasy with the smoking destruction. Dagger waited, tail swishing.

Justice called out again to the men and was answered only by silence. A fat cloud drifted high overhead. Its shadow trailed after it, a patch of darkness sliding across the bleak landscape.

The dog came up to Justice and uncharacteristically leaned against him. Just as uncharacteristically, Justice smoothed a hand over the animal's wiry fur.

"What happened here, boy? Where are Hector and Jorge?"

It didn't make much sense talking to a dog, but Justice reckoned these were questions he didn't need to ask anyone anyway. He knew the answers.

Circling the burnt-out home, he eventually spotted the charred and twisted remains of both men. There wasn't much left of them, but it was enough to confirm his suspicions.

Hector and his son had died defending Nora's ranch, which Tucker—probably by the hand of Del Mundo—had burned anyway.

He panned his vision across the charred shells that had only yesterday been a barn and new stable.

So much destruction. And for what? So a wealthy cattle baron could have more acres, more water, more cattle?

Whatever the case, none of that mattered anymore.

What was done was done. The only thing left to do was to see justice served.

He had been foolishly holding onto the hope that the new cattleman's association might, through a show of unified strength, put Tucker in check and bring him to his senses.

Justice had never lifted the death sentence he had imposed on Del Mundo, but he had begun to hope that maybe Nora, Diego, and the other small ranchers of this valley might be able to avoid the apocalyptic bloodshed of an all-out range war.

Now, however, he knew the truth. Neither Nora nor Diego nor any other would ever know peace in this valley until they established true justice.

"I'm sorry, my friends," he told the charred remains of Hector and Jorge, "but you will have your vengeance. I promise you that. You will have your vengeance."

He handed the dog a fistful of jerky and patted it on the head. "Stay here, boy. I'll be back."

Then he headed for Dos Pesos.

Manuel Chavez was surprised to see Justice return to the livery. He smiled. "Did you reconsider my offer to buy that beautiful horse?"

Justice shook his head. He said nothing about what had happened, but Chavez must've read some of it in his countenance, because suddenly, the hostler was all business.

Justice told him what he wanted and paid, including an extra dollar. "Swap out my saddle, will you? I'll be back for the fresh horse soon."

He strode down the street and a short time later entered the sheriff's office, where a young deputy told him that Perkins was over at the inn getting a late lunch.

"Get ready to ride, son. You're fixing to earn your pay."

With no further explanation Justice walked out the door and went into the Dos Pesos Hotel, where he merely nodded at the woman who greeted him and headed straight into the dining room and immediately spotted Sheriff Perkins, bibbed and smiling, halfway through a savory meal.

Perkins looked up. Seeing Justice, his smile died.

"Time's up," Justice said.

The other diners all stared at him.

"What do you mean?" Perkins asked as the color drained from his face. "What happened?"

"They burned my ranch and killed my men. Now, I'm heading over there to set things right. Time. Is. Up."

The sheriff blinked up at him with bulging eyes.

"You gotta choose, Sheriff. Right now."

CHAPTER 35

"All right, men," Justice said, several hours later when the ranchers and their punchers had gathered together at the southern edge of Diego's ranch. "It's time to take this valley back."

A few ranchers had backed out at the last minute, but most were present, and Justice liked what he saw on their faces: not fear, not elation, but stony resignation.

"Remember," he said, "we're riding down to seek justice not to burn them out."

"They put up a fight, we'll sure burn them out," one of the ranchers, a tough man name Robles, declared.

"It's a last resort. I think they'll fight. Question is how much fight do they have in them? If it comes to shooting, shoot to kill. But let's not turn this into a senseless massacre is all I'm saying."

Men nodded, seeming to appreciate the sentiment. All told there were twenty-one ranchers and thirty-five cowpunchers.

Many would not be true fighters, but all were armed.

They could point and shoot, anyway, and some had experience.

Justice liked the odds.

"We're gonna split up into three crews. Dave, you take two dozen men and ride to the left. Jed, you take another two dozen and ride to the right. Dave, you come in from the east. Jed, you come from the west and try to wrap around to the back of the house."

Jed nodded. "Where you gonna be, Justice?"

"I'm coming right down the middle. Sheriff Perkins, you ride with me."

The sheriff nodded.

Justice was glad the man had chosen to ride along. It wasn't just about having an extra gun or legitimizing their cause, though those things did matter very much.

What also mattered about Perkins's decision was the impact it would have on his life.

If he had tucked tail and run, he would have spent the rest of his days branded as a coward and hating himself.

Justice reckoned that Perkins, like many lawmen in these wild territories, had underestimated the challenges of their positions and gotten in over their heads. He wasn't a bad man. He was just overwhelmed.

Tonight was his chance to redeem himself and start over as a respected lawman.

Perkins said, "You men heard Mr. Justice. We're riding in the name of setting things right not murder."

"If Tucker won't come out, Sheriff Perkins and I are going in. We could use a few men with experience to ride with us. I'm not asking who out there is brave or can shoot. I need a few volunteers who've fought with guns before."

Diego and Chester, both Civil War veterans, brought their horses forward.

So did a middle-aged black man named Aaron Biscoe.

Justice didn't know Biscoe well but did know he had served in the Civil War. After the war, Biscoe became a buffalo soldier on the frontier. Judging by the look in his eyes, he had seen plenty of combat.

"I don't know, Diego," Chester laughed. "You reckon we ought to let this blue belly ride with us?"

"I don't know, Chester. Maybe? I mean the war's over."

This banter earned a slight grin from Biscoe. "You boys just get ready to scream that womanly rebel yell of yours, and I'll do all the real fighting."

While the ranchers and their hands split into two large groups, a lone man far too young to have fought in the war also rode forward.

The man was compact, probably only 5'5" with broad shoulders and boxy hands. His chest stuck out like that of a fighting rooster. But his face, with its hard, dark eyes set close to its beaklike nose, was all desert hawk.

"I can fight," he told Justice.

"What's your name?" Justice asked, recognizing him only as a puncher for Beau "Poppy" Shartelle, a rancher who had shouted about Tucker but ultimately proved too cowardly to join the fight.

"Coronado."

"All right, Coronado," Justice said, shaking his hand. "Glad to have you along."

"Let's light torches and put the fear of God into 'em," somebody suggested.

"Not unless you want them to put lead into you," Justice replied. "A man with a torch is an easy target. Riding in under cover of darkness is an advantage, gentlemen. They are defending, which is an enviable position. We need every advantage we can get. Let's ride."

They trotted through the night, saving their horses for the final action.

They met with no resistance as they crossed into Tucker's land and continued unmolested until they topped a rise and rode out of a stand of ponderosas overlooking a massive ranch house with lots of glass and heavy timber, a monstrosity that would have looked more at home in some Eastern resort than here in this land of sand and scrub and adobe homes. It was all lit up like Tucker was hosting a party.

And he is hosting a party, Justice thought. *He just doesn't know it yet.*

As they left the trees they split into their three predetermined groups.

Dave and his men went left, while Jed and his riders veered off in the opposite direction. Both forces stuck to the edge of the trees and slowed their approach as planned, buying time for Justice and his men to try a more diplomatic approach.

"Men ahead," Aaron Biscoe reported. "Behind that gate."

Justice squinted, and the sentries came into view. A fence surrounded the ten or fifteen acres immediately surrounding Tucker's mansion, and he had apparently posted two guards at his front gate.

Justice's riders spread out forming an arrowhead with Justice on point.

He was just getting ready to hail the gate when one of the sentries shouted. A second later one guard opened fire while the other mounted up and headed downhill toward Tucker's mansion, riding for all he was worth.

Justice returned fire, as did the men to either side of him, and the sentry who'd shot at them dropped to the ground.

When they reached the fence Coronado rushed forward, dismounted nimbly, and opened the gate.

They charged downhill after the mounted sentry, who reached the house and ran up its broad steps, shouting to those inside.

A moment later, men poured from the doors onto the timber deck. Bottles and flasks winked in most of their hands.

They're celebrating the raid, Justice thought. *Celebrating the murder of my friends.*

Some of the men ran back inside. Others dropped their bottles, pulled sidearms, and started firing wildly at Justice and his riders.

So much for diplomacy, he thought, as his friends returned fire.

Dave and his men came howling out of the eastern darkness, muzzles flashing. A second later Jed's troop opened fire, charging from the right, sweeping along the western side of the house, raking it with gunfire as they wrapped around to the back where more gunfire sounded.

A few men dropped on the deck boards, dead or hit hard. The other defenders retreated. Behind them those who'd retreated earlier returned, rifles in hand, and stood at windows and in doorways firing into the darkness.

Fifty yards from the short set of broad stairs, Justice dismounted, hauled his Winchester from its boot, and slapped the rented gelding on its rump, sending it away into the relative safety of the outer darkness.

There was no cover here, save the cover of darkness, so he ran forward as quickly as he could, zigging and zagging, and fired his rifle when he reached the deck.

A man fell away from the window.

As soon as he pulled the trigger, Justice moved again. A good thing, too, as several defenders fired at the spot where they'd seen his muzzle flash.

He moved along the deck, popped up, and fired again, even as the men with him did the same.

The defender's gunfire slowed, giving Justice time to lean his rifle against a deck post and unsling and open his haversack. From it he retrieved the item Sheriff Huff had helped him procure in Santa Fe.

Justice scratched a match to life, lit the fuse, and waited, as gunshots cracked overhead.

When only a few seconds of fuse remained, he hurled the bundle of dynamite over the deck and through the open front door of the house.

CHAPTER 36

As the battle was beginning, Haversham started shrieking like a hysterical woman.

Tucker slapped the tiny lawyer across the face, knocking his spectacles askew.

Haversham clapped one of his pale, womanly hands to the pink mark on his cheek and stared at Tucker with a shocked expression.

It was all Tucker could do not to laugh at the namby-pamby little Easterner. "Get yourself together, Haversham. This is no time for whimpering. It's time for action."

Haversham nodded and straightened his spectacles.

"Here," Tucker said, holding out a Colt revolver to Haversham.

The prissy lawyer took a step back and raised his soft hands to his chest, fluttering them back and forth and staring at the pistol like it might bite him. "I am an educated man, Mr. Tucker, not a savage. I refuse to use those implements of destruction. Besides, if these ruffians breach your inner sanctum and see that thing in my hands, they will gun me down."

"You and all your education are about as useful as thumbs on a chicken now, Haversham. What are you going to do, talk them to death? At least Pearl had the sense to take the gun I gave her. Do you want to go hide behind her skirts?"

"No sir. I might not be a fighter, but I won't abandon you. I will stay by your side no matter what. And though you disparage my education, I will indeed try to reason with these men if they come in here seeking to harm you."

"Pshaw! Lot of good that'll do. When men are out for blood there are no substitutes. Not words or gold or even women. This ends here, tonight, in blood, winner take all."

As he spoke, Tucker swiveled behind his massive mahogany desk and started pulling firearms from the wall cabinet. He laid several rifles and three double-barreled shot-guns, all loaded, atop the desk, their muzzles facing the double doors across the room.

There wasn't much room behind the huge C-shaped desk, and that was by design. He didn't want anyone flanking him and coming in from behind. As long as he could keep his enemies in front of him, he would have a distinct advantage.

Tucker pushed the chair aside and took its place. He would make his last stand here.

"Well, get back here with me if you're going to stay, Haversham."

Haversham hesitated, blinking at the tight space behind the desk. "Won't we be trapped, sir?"

"No, we'll be safe. See, what these men don't understand is that my desk is reinforced with steel plates." Tucker grinned at Haversham's obvious amazement. "It's bullet-proofed. Now, I might not be educated, but I am experienced. Life among ruthless men prepared me for this moment, and I am ready, lucky for you, my squirrelly little lawyer. We will hide behind this bulletproof desk, and they will have no cover whatsoever. They'll have to come through those doors into a steady rain of lead."

Downstairs the gunfire increased. The raiders had drawn close to the house, and Tucker's defenders were fighting hard to protect him.

Good. That was good.

But he was still confused.

"I must confess that I am surprised," Tucker said, selecting one of the lever-action Winchester repeaters, a good weapon to start with, given that it provided plenty of rounds and plenty of firepower. He'd save the shotguns in case the invaders managed to get closer. "With that silent justice dead, I didn't think the ranchers would dare to attack. But here they are."

"I am surprised, too, sir—shocked, even. Perhaps they gathered strength from his death, like zealots inspired by a martyr."

Tucker shrugged. "Whatever the case, they're here now, and we gotta make martyrs out of every last one of them. Once this shakes out there will be no mercy, no survivors, and no witnesses. We're gonna wipe the River Valley Cattleman's Association off the map. Then we'll take a ride. It isn't work I like, you understand, but we've gotta go all the way tonight. No witnesses."

Haversham shuddered. "You don't mean, sir…"

"Yes, that's exactly what I mean. We have to wipe out every man, woman, and child who stood against us. There's a lesson they won't teach you in your fancy law school. In moments like these, never do anything by half measure. You let the women and kids go, the next thing you know you'll have a whole cavalry regiment coming for you. That won't do. You gotta go all the way. Go big, go bold, and win everything."

The doors banged open, and Tucker raised the rifle.

A bewildered Del Mundo stood in the doorway looking around the room. His frightened eyes finally found Tucker behind the desk. With the doors open the sounds of the gun battle were greatly increased.

"What in tarnation is wrong with you, Del Mundo? I almost shot you dead."

"Sir, it isn't even possible but…"

"Spit it out, Del Mundo!"

"Justice… he's here."

"How is that even possible? You said you killed him."

"I did, sir. I killed him… twice. But he's outside. I saw him kill Del Peterson."

"Well, you're just going to have to kill him again," Tucker said, and pointed at Del Mundo's pistol. "Wait for him in the den. No man can survive a .45 at close range."

"Okay sir, but I'm starting to think maybe he can't be—"

"Shut your mouth, Del Mundo. Don't even put your crazy ideas into words, you hear me? Justice is your mess, Del Mundo. You clean it up."

Del Mundo blinked at his Colt then nodded. "Yes sir. I'll kill him again. I just hope he stays dead this time. At least long enough for me to get out of New Mexico Territory."

Del Mundo walked out and closed the doors behind him. Tucker felt good about placing him just down the hall, very good indeed.

Meanwhile, the fighting grew even louder downstairs.

Tucker shook his head, shouldered the rifle, and laid its barrel across the bulletproof desk, ready to make his stand. "Sounds like they brought a veritable army with them. As you can see, Haversham, I readied a good number of weapons to defend our position, but now I'm thinking I might need your help. Don't have a heart attack, you pansy. I know you don't have the sand to fight, but can I at least count on you to reload weapons once I've emptied them?"

Haversham nodded, his eyes huge and strange, as he sidled behind Tucker. "You can count on me, sir."

Then, downstairs, a deafening explosion rocked the house.

CHAPTER 37

T he bundled dynamite detonated, rocking the house and sending a volley of debris overhead.

Justice slung his rifle over one shoulder, drew his Colt, and charged forward crunching over glass and hopping the many bodies that littered the heavy timbers of the deck.

A massive hole gaped in the face of the house, partially obscured by a cloud of dark smoke. Here and there, curtains and clothing burned.

Justice plunged through the smoke, followed closely by Coronado, who held a pistol in each hand, and Biscoe, who wielded a short, double-barreled shotgun. Behind them came Perkins and the old rebels, Diego and Chester, with rifles at the ready.

Most of the first floor was given over to a high-vaulted great room, where Tucker had no doubt intended to entertain the region's wealthy and powerful after eradicating these pesky small-time ranchers. Now the once great hall was a bloody battlefield, men fighting on all sides, bodies everywhere.

A bearded man popped up from behind an overturned

couch and fired at Justice, who returned fire, hitting the man in the middle of his chest and putting him down.

Seeing no sign of Del Mundo or Tucker, Justice ran to an open set of stairs, vaulting over bodies and exchanging gunfire with another ill-fated defender.

At the foot of the stairs he holstered his six-shooter, which had only one round remaining, and unslung his Winchester, which still contained seven rounds by his count.

He rushed to the top of the stairs but paused at the top to check every direction.

Looking back he saw Chester Robinson through a haze of smoke. The old confederate gave a bloodcurdling yell and charged forward, firing his rifle.

One of Tucker's men fell.

Another stepped from behind a column and shot Chester point blank in the back of the head.

Justice swung his rifle, filled his sights with the man who'd killed his friend, and pulled the trigger. The bullet tore through his neck, avenging the fallen rancher.

He swung the barrel, shot another defender and then another. A bullet smashed into the ceiling near his head, and Justice fired again, knocking another of Tucker's men from his feet.

He leaned into the upstairs hallway and whipped his head back just in time as both barrels of a shotgun boomed, obliterating the door frame where through which he'd peeked only a second before.

He fell into a crouch, leaned into the hall and fired, jacked the lever, and fired again, killing the man who'd been trying to reload his shotgun.

Where was Tucker?

Where was Del Mundo for that matter?

Del Mundo was here somewhere, but from the outlaw's actions at the Lopez place, Justice knew he feared death. Del

Mundo wouldn't come out and face Justice like a man. No, he would lie fearfully in wait, hoping to get the jump on him. Justice moved forward with extra caution, expecting a trap.

The killing calm was on Justice now, but the men he truly wanted dead were evading him.

He had only one round remaining in his rifle and knew it was time to reload. But then his eyes went to the pistol riding in the holster of the man he'd killed.

Knowing it would be faster to grab that pistol than reload his own, Justice rushed forward.

At that second, Del Mundo stepped from a doorway near the end of the hall and fired his pistol.

A line of fire burned across the side of Justice's head as a bullet grazed him.

Justice fired his last round, punching Del Mundo in the shoulder and knocking him backward several steps. The outlaw's pistol went flying.

Roaring with pain and rage, the burly redhead yanked a Bowie from its sheathe.

Justice smiled and walked calmly forward. Some part of him wanted to throw down the rifle and pull his own blade, but he knew this was no time for fun, only business.

"You!" Del Mundo shouted, his face twisting with horror. "I already killed you… twice!"

"And now I'm going to kill you," Justice said, advancing on the terrified man, gripping the rifle in both hands.

Del Mundo slashed the air wildly.

Justice evaded the blade, surged forward, and slammed the butt of the rifle into Del Mundo's jaw.

The burly outlaw staggered backward, braced himself, and rushed forward, thrusting his knife at Justice's abdomen.

Justice sidestepped, parrying the blade with the butt of his rifle, then whacked the barrel sharply down on Del Mundo's nose, which shattered beneath the blow.

Del Mundo bellowed with pain and bulled forward, but Justice launched a rear leg kick that slammed into Del Mundo's meaty thigh and checked his charge.

Del Mundo lunged awkwardly, trying again to skewer him with the knife.

This time Justice was ready. Dropping the rifle he side-stepped the attack, seized Del Mundo's wrist, hauled the big man forward, and drilled him in the gut with his knee in the same technique he had displayed in the office of Santa Fe's sheriff, J.T. Huff.

A second later, he bent Del Mundo's wrist backward, clutched the freckled hand, and drove the knife into the murderer's side once, twice, three times.

Del Mundo cried out, flailing uselessly. He surrendered the knife and turned, bellowing, trying to latch onto Justice's throat, but Justice whipped the knife upward with a tight uppercut, burying it to the hilt in the bad man's solar plexus.

Del Mundo reeled backward with a gasp and fell on his backside, hard, blinked with disbelief, and eased back into death.

Without delay Justice dropped the knife and set to reloading his Colt, which he gripped as he approached the big double doors at the end of the hall.

Talk about a death trap. Tucker was probably waiting on the other side of those doors with a shotgun.

Justice wished he had more dynamite.

Before trying the double doors he paused outside the last room on the right, knowing Tucker could just as easily be hiding inside it.

Justice kicked through the door and dipped aside just in time. From within sounded a feminine cry and a loud double shot, two triggers pulled practically at once.

He leaned back in putting his barrel on the pretty, dark-haired woman weeping beside a large bed.

"Ma'am, kindly put away that firearm before you get yourself killed. You have nothing to fear from us unless you foolishly attack again."

Without waiting for her reply he pressed forward, shouldered through the double doors, and dropped into a crouch, pistol at the ready.

The expected blast of gunfire never came.

A large man was slumped across the surface of a massive mahogany desk, his outstretched hands still gripping a rifle.

Was that Tucker?

Justice supposed so, based on the man's size and bushy sideburns. Justice might have suspected a trap if the man weren't so clearly dead. There was blood everywhere, and the back of Tucker's head was a mess.

Haversham lay on the floor to Justice's right. He was unarmed, covered in blood, and weeping hysterically. "Mr. Justice? Oh, I am so happy to see you, sir. Del Mundo came in here and murdered Mr. Tucker and shot me as well. I need a doctor, sir. Please help me. Please, sir!"

Justice ignored him, advancing slowly and cautiously toward the huge desk of the dead rancher, still wanting to make completely sure that the big Texan was truly dead.

His gut shouted at him.

Something wasn't right here.

Why would Del Mundo shoot Tucker in the back of the head?

Sure, the outlaw might turn on the man, but if he did, he'd gun him down while looking him in the eyes.

Also, why would Tucker let a man like Del Mundo get behind him in a moment like this?

Besides, a man of Del Mundo's size wouldn't even fit behind Tucker there, would he? No. Only a much smaller man could fit in a space that tight, a man as small as...

Justice dropped into a crouch and spun just as the Colt roared behind him.

He fired, nailing the murderous lawyer just above the belt buckle, then pulled the trigger again, adding another hole a few inches higher.

The bullets blew Haversham off his feet. The revolver he'd used to try to shoot Justice in the back of the head landed several feet away. The venomous lawyer lay there groaning and coughing.

Justice stood and walked over, ready to fire again if need be.

Turned out, there was no need.

"You… killed… me," Haversham gasped, his terrified eyes filling the lenses of his wire-rimmed spectacles. "Guess it's true… what they say… about… silent justices. Oh, how I… hate… the West."

And with that, Haversham died.

CHAPTER 38

A second later Coronado entered the room, ready to fight alongside Justice.

The men nodded at each other, Justice figuring Coronado was a good man to have beside you in a fight.

Diego and Sheriff Perkins joined them several seconds later.

Perkins's left arm hung limp at his side, sheathed in blood, but Justice had never seen the sheriff's face so alive.

"You okay, Justice?" Diego asked.

Justice nodded. "You?"

Diego nodded. "Chester Robinson, though—"

"I saw what happened," Justice said. "Shame. He was a good man."

"A lot of good men rode in here tonight," Diego said. "Fewer will be riding home."

"We fared better than Tucker's men," Coronado said.

"He started it, we finished it," Justice said. "You can't stop men from doing evil. You just have to stop them from continuing to do more."

"That is the truth," Perkins said. "Diego's right. We took

losses. Bill Elliot and Elias Flores are gone. Jake Cavit, too, if I'm not mistaken. We have several men wounded, some seriously, as well, but law and order prevailed, gentlemen. Law and order prevailed."

Coronado shrugged. "I'm just glad we won."

And won they had. Downstairs, the battle was over.

Justice and his friends quickly checked the spacious office for anyone who might be hiding concealed within closets, cabinets, or curtains.

They found no one but the dead.

Diego paused beside Tucker's massive desk scanning a piece of paper there. He picked it up and handed it to Justice. "I think this might be talking about you, my friend."

It was a telegram.

SULLIVAN TUCKER, DOS PESOS, NEW MEXICO TERRITORY – SJ heading your way from Colorado (stop) Cochran missed (stop) SJ could ruin everything (stop) Counting on you (stop) Take care of him (stop) Otherwise, I will send Rose (stop) D.G.

JUSTICE READ IT AND REREAD IT.

SJ.

Silent Justice.

Who were these men? This D.G. clearly controlled Tucker and had just as clearly called for Justice's execution.

There's a man I need to meet, Justice thought. *Pronto.*

"Sheriff Perkins," a deep voice said, and Aaron Biscoe entered the room escorting the dark-haired woman who'd tried to kill Justice. "You'll want to watch this one. She don't look particularly dangerous, but when I was clearing rooms she came at me with a pen knife."

The former buffalo soldier turned his head and showed the nasty gash bleeding on his cheek, just an inch from his eye.

"Mrs. Tucker, I presume?" Justice said, sizing up the vicious little woman.

"I wish to speak with my lawyer, please."

"That works," Justice said. "Unless Haversham was your lawyer. He is indefinitely indisposed."

"My lawyer is Mr. J.P. Woodrow of the great state of Texas, thank you very much. I wouldn't have that snake Haversham for my lawyer. He was a horrible man, much like my husband, much like all of these horrible men."

"Sheriff Perkins, you'll want to cuff this lady," Justice said. "Before coming at Mr. Biscoe with a pen knife, she tried to blow my head off with a derringer. Let her rot in your jail until her lawyer shows up from Texas… if he shows up at all."

"Gladly," Perkins said, holstering his sidearm and pulling handcuffs from his belt.

Mrs. Tucker looked shocked but did not resist. Still, it took some of the starch out of her. "Sir," she said to Justice, "please allow me to apologize. You must understand that I was frightened for my life."

"That's understandable," Justice said, wanting to work with her, needing her help to understand the big picture here. "There was a lot of shooting going on."

"Yes," she said, nodding emphatically. "That is the truth, Sheriff. This man has recognized the truth."

"Duly noted," Perkins said.

"One thing I don't understand, Mrs. Tucker," Justice said.

"Please, call me Pearl." She offered a sickly-sweet smile, finally realizing, perhaps, that these men held her fate in their hands. "When you say *Mrs. Tucker*, I feel you are addressing some unfortunate woman I never met."

This girl's a pretty hard customer, Justice thought, but

outwardly, he merely nodded. "All right then, Pearl, you clearly were not happy here. Why hitch your wagon to Tucker in the first place?"

"Mr. Tucker lured me out of Texas with all number of false promises. He made it sound like he was a very important man, a very powerful man, but it was all a sham, Mr. Justice. He didn't own this ranch or even run these men, not really."

"Who did?"

She blinked at him looking suddenly frightened, a strange thing to see in a woman so coldly unaffected by the death of her husband. "That, I cannot say. Mr. Tucker, Mr. Haversham, and to some degree that filthy barbarian Mr. Del Mundo each had his own agenda, and they were all working against one another in some capacity, all angling to take control of this ranch and all the wealth it afforded. Not that Mr. Haversham wanted to become a rancher. He just wanted money so he could start over in some big city."

"Why would Haversham murder Tucker?" Justice asked, getting to the question he really wanted to ask.

Pearl Tucker gave her dead husband a condescending smile and shook her head. "Mr. Tucker never understood how dangerous Mr. Haversham really was. Men are always like that. They don't listen, they don't see. They want what they want, and they stick to it like bloodhounds on a fresh trail. I, on the other hand, had the sense to watch and listen when these men talked. I think I was the only one who actually heard what they were all saying, the only one who understood what they all wanted." She gave a bitter laugh. "And the whole time they thought of me as a stupid female. But where are they now, Mr. Justice? Dead, that's where. Meanwhile, their stupid female is still here."

"Well, Pearl, I certainly don't think you're stupid," Justice said. "You were lied to and taken out of Texas but still managed to survive in this place."

This seemed to please his would-be murderess. "Why thank you for saying that, Mr. Justice."

"Just stating the facts as I see them, ma'am. But I do wonder, how would murdering Mr. Tucker help Mr. Haversham reach his goal? I'm missing something here."

Pearl laughed a high-pitched and decidedly unpleasant titter. "You, Mr. Justice. You are missing *you*. Don't you understand? You were the key to Mr. Haversham's fortune."

CHAPTER 39

J ustice raised one eyebrow, letting his confusion show plainly on his face. "I apologize, ma'am, but I'm not following you."

"Mr. Tucker did not like Mr. Haversham. If Mr. Tucker had conquered this valley and killed you in the process, he would have solidified his claim in New Mexico and would have lived like an emperor. He would have dismissed Haversham outright. Or perhaps even killed him.

"Whatever the case, if Mr. Tucker had won this battle, Mr. Haversham would have been finished. On the other hand, if Mr. Tucker died and Mr. Haversham was able to kill you, the dreaded silent justice, well, he would have escaped this mess looking like a very valuable asset indeed. Mr. Haversham gambled… and lost."

"He sure did. Thank you for explaining that to me."

"Hold on a tick," Perkins said, looking at Justice with wide eyes. "You're a silent justice?"

"I was."

"What's that?" Diego asked.

Perkins laughed incredulously. "Stuff of legends, that's what. The ultimate lawman."

Justice ignored him. "Pearl, what I'm really hoping to figure out is who is really in control here?" He swept the telegram from the desk and held it up for her to read. As her eyes flicked back and forth, the color drained from her face. "Who are D.G. and Rose?"

Pearl's eyes bulged. "I'm certain I have no idea what you are talking about, Mr. Justice. No idea at all."

"That's a lie," Perkins said, stepping forward. "I might remind you, Mrs. Tucker, that the judges in this territory hang women, too. You are in a heap of trouble here. You help us now, and things might go better for you. Perhaps even much better."

"Sheriff Perkins," Pearl said, "with all due respect, I put very little faith in any of your threats or promises. You are cut of the same cloth as Mr. Tucker and Mr. Haversham, a man of no character merely looking out for himself."

Justice figured maybe she was wrong about Perkins. Before Perkins had ridden in here, Pearl's description would have fit him perfectly. But Perkins was a man transformed and, Justice hoped, a man redeemed.

Whatever the case, Pearl would not trust Perkins, so Justice spoke up. He had completed his vengeance upon his four murderers, but now that he understood that murder had been ordered from afar, he very much wanted to track down these other men. "Excuse me, Pearl, but what if I gave my word that helping us would improve your chances? As it stands, you face an assault charge for your attack on Mr. Biscoe and a very serious charge of attempted murder for trying to shoot me. If I were to retract my complaint—and I assure you that I will if you lead me to whoever runs this operation—you would face only the assault charge, though I suspect Mr. Biscoe might be willing to drop that as well."

He glanced at Biscoe, who nodded. "She gives you what you need, it's water under the bridge as far as I'm concerned."

Justice smiled. "Tell us who D.G. and Rose are, and you'll be a free woman tonight."

Pearl shook her head. "I do appreciate the offer, Mr. Justice, and I do trust your word and that of Mr. Biscoe, but I must nonetheless decline. What good is freedom if I'm dead?"

"We're not talking bail here," Perkins said. "That's the point. Give us the information, and I'll unlock these cuffs, take you to the hotel, and make sure you have enough money to get back to Texas. You'll be free to start over."

Pearl shook her head. "You have no idea who you're dealing with, do you? I'm sorry, gentlemen. But I will say nothing and put my faith in my lawyer, Mr. J.P. Woodrow. If I provide the names and information you are requesting, my death would come swiftly, and when it arrived I would beg for the mercy of a hangman's noose. No, this mystery you will have to unravel yourselves. I will not say another word."

"All right," Perkins said. "It's your funeral."

"I am willing to help in other ways," Pearl said. "For example, I would be willing to share the name of the other man who wanted you dead, Mr. Justice."

"All right," Justice said.

"Will you drop your charge against me?"

"Maybe. I gotta hear what you have to say."

"That's not good enough. I need your word that you'll drop the charge against me, Mr. Justice." Her eyes flicked around the room as if she were seeking an escape route. Then, locking her gaze on a section of wood paneling, she smiled. "Tucker's money! I can give you Tucker's money. There's a safe in that wall. State of the art, very difficult to crack. But I can give you the combination."

"All right," Justice said.

"Give me your word, please."

"You have my word, Pearl, that if you tell me who else was trying to kill me and give us the combination to the safe, I won't press charges."

"The other man referred to in the telegram is Ruble Cochran. He's one more hungry wolf like these other men," she said, gesturing coldly to the bodies that surrounded them, "though in all fairness to Mr. Cochran, he has bigger teeth and knows how to run his pack."

And yet she doesn't fear him like the other two, Justice thought. Interesting. "Where can I find him."

"Leadville."

Justice nodded, unsurprised. Leadville was a wild town, perfect for organized crime. "Thank you for that, Pearl," Justice said. "Now, how about that safe combination?"

She was good to her word on that count, too.

When they opened the safe and looked inside, they saw bundles of greenbacks and stacks of gold coins.

Coronado whistled. "That's a lot of money."

"Sorry, boys," Perkins said, "but this is a crime scene. I'll be confiscating that."

"No," Justice said, stepping between Perkins and the safe, "you won't."

"What's this?" Perkins said. "I thought you were a lawman."

"Perhaps I was a lawman, but that life ended when I died. I am no longer the law. Now, I am justice."

"But they're the same thing."

Justice shook his head. "The law is about rules. Justice is about truth. And the truth of this situation is that Tucker hurt a lot of people. The Lopezes, for example. And Nora Eckert. Hector and Jorge Barrera, Chester Robinson, Bill Elliot, Elias Flores, Jake Cavit, and everyone else who got hurt or killed tonight, along with their families and anyone whose cattle has been rustled over recent months. This money will go to these folks. For those hit hardest, it won't bring back their loved ones, but it will give the survivors a shot at still getting by."

Perkins blinked at him a few times then nodded.

"That might not be the law," Justice said, "but it is right, and it is justice."

CHAPTER 40

A month later Justice, Nora, and Diego sat in the office of their lawyer, David Spencer, who smiled and said, "We won. The Casterlin Corporation has surrendered all cattle as we proposed in exchange for our dropping all charges. I still believe they would have won if they had pushed back, but they cared more about staying out of the papers than they did those cattle."

Justice figured the corporation had made a smart move.

The deed to Tucker's sprawling ranch had belonged to the Casterlin Corporation of New York, New York. Hypothetically, that made them liable for criminal activities under Tucker's watch, especially because stolen livestock were identified among the herds grazing their land.

Why had a mysterious New York City corporation purchased this massive ranch in New Mexico and flooded it with 7000 head of cattle?

"It's a strange corporation," David Spencer said. "The membership is private, and nobody would tell me exactly what they do. I did discover connections to railroads, mining, and lumber, but I believe the corporation's primary

208

function is to protect the identity, activity, and income of its members, whoever they might be."

Someday, Justice reckoned, he would investigate this shadowy corporation, but for now, he wanted to uncover his past and get on with his future.

"We thought they might give us the cows," Diego told Spencer.

"And what has the River Valley Cattleman's Association decided to do," Spencer asked. "Sell them off?"

"Branded animals have already been returned to their rightful owners," Nora explained. "The remainder of the cattle would be portioned out equally among everyone who rode against Tucker."

"Everyone?"

"Well, everyone but Perkins," Justice said. "That would represent a conflict of interests."

Spencer looked back and forth between them, smiling. "But everyone else gets an equal share of the cattle?"

They nodded.

"This is going to make for some very happy cowpunchers."

"Those men risked everything riding with us," Justice said.

"And some of them never rode home," Diego said solemnly.

"I respect your decision," Spencer said. "In fact, I applaud it. I just hadn't expected it. Such magnanimity is not common in these parts. Don't get me wrong. People are nice enough, but there's something like a caste system in place here. It's not easy for a cowpoke to get ahead."

"Well, we got some that are about to get ahead," Justice said.

"Way ahead," Nora agreed.

Each man who'd ridden against Tucker would gain

roughly 120 head of cattle—a value of over $3000—a massive payday for the ranchers and nothing short of a miracle to the cowhands, most of whom worked for a dollar a day and had probably never owned much more than what they could stuff in a saddlebag or tuck in a bedroll.

"What about the acreage?" Diego asked.

"All 243,007 acres will be signed over to the River Valley Cattleman's Association," Spencer said.

Nora beamed. "That is truly wonderful news."

"Has the association already decided what it wants to do with the land?" Spencer asked.

"Yes," Nora said. "The River Valley Cattleman's Association will offer each of the hands who'd fought a 2000-acre parcel, so long as the men agree to join the association and stand ready to defend the valley again."

Justice did not bother to explain that he, too, would gain a 2000-acre parcel adjoining Nora's land. He would put her name on the deed, too, in case anything happened to him, and then they'd just see what they'd do after he chased down his past.

Spencer laughed happily. "This is going to be fun to watch. I keep picturing that old penny pincher Fester Quartey. He didn't ride with you, did he?"

Now it was Diego's turn to laugh. "He did not. Said it was none of his business. My guess is the man will die of bitterness when he hears the news."

"It's in the association's best interest," Justice explained. "By giving these men land and cattle, we'll create dozens of new ranches owned by men willing to fight for the common cause."

"What if they want to sell?" Spencer asked. "I can't imagine some of these cowboys wanting to settle down."

"We'll need your help with the paperwork," Nora said. "We want to include a provision that says they may only sell to ranchers who agree to join and cooperate with the cattleman's association."

"And what about the rest of the land? That must leave close to 200,000 acres unaccounted for."

"173,007 acres," Diego said. "That will be commonly owned amounting to open range for members of the association."

"We can put it to a vote later if we want to sell any or all of that ground," Nora added.

"I can see you've really thought this through," Spencer said.

"Not just us," Diego said. "The whole association. Well, those who rode, anyway. Some of the sessions got downright boisterous, but we ended up sorting things out."

They explained to Spencer in confidence what they had done with the money they'd gotten from Tucker.

The association would use some of the money to rebuild Tucker's house, which they would use as an official headquarters. The escrowed money would pay for a caretaker and any necessary upkeep, along with the monthly gatherings scheduled to be held there for members of the association and special guests like Justice and Sheriff Perkins, who was, indeed, a changed man.

Most of the money, however, went to widows and those who'd suffered major property loss.

The association had given Nora $1500, more than enough to build and supply a very nice ranch house and all necessary outbuildings.

None of the Lopezes had ridden against Tucker, of course, but Diego made the point that Roberto would have ridden if he'd been well.

Besides, Justice had pointed out, Mrs. Lopez already shot up Tucker's men.

The cattlemen had gotten a good laugh out of that. Then they'd voted unanimously to help the Lopezes.

Since then, the Lopezes had moved back onto their plot. Roberto was recovering well. He would always have a limp, but with the money Tucker had paid them, they could now afford to build a bunkhouse and hire on a few hands to oversee not only the cattle that had been returned to them but also the 120 additional head they would soon gain. They were incredibly grateful to Justice and the others who had given them a way to keep their dream alive.

For others, of course, there was no rebuilding of dreams. Hector and Jorge were dead, and with no immediate family, that was the end of their sad story, a truth that would haunt Justice till his dying day. He was happy to have avenged their murders, but that did little to change the hard, cold facts of their deaths.

But that's the way life was. And that went double for life in the West. Some things, money couldn't put right.

Some things would never be right. Others had to be put right by hand.

Shortly after taking care of Tucker, Justice received a telegram from Santa Fe.

MR. JUSTICE, DOS PESOS, NEW MEXICO TERRITORY – HAVE confirmed likely existence of silent justices (stop) Sources say never more than eleven in total. (stop) Rumored head-quarters in Texas, possibly Austin (stop) Also rumored presidential appointment (stop) Happy hunting (stop) Sheriff J.T. Huff, Santa Fe

IT WASN'T MUCH TO GO ON, BUT JUSTICE WAS THANKFUL FOR

Huff's help. He sent a telegram saying so and summing up the situation with Tucker.

Huff responded again.

MR. JUSTICE, DOS PESOS, NEW MEXICO TERRITORY – Concerning Ruble Cochran of Leadville (stop) Man of some influence and reputation (stop) Owns multiple saloons, bordellos, and gambling houses including The Gilded Lily (stop). Known to employ the worst of men (stop) Proceed with caution (stop) Happy hunting (stop) Sheriff J.T. Huff, Santa Fe

JUSTICE WAS THANKFUL FOR THIS NEW INFORMATION. ONCE Nora's new house was built and everything was in order, he would travel to Leadville and track down Cochran, who had apparently tried to kill him and served, as had Tucker, the mysterious D.G.

These people would pay for their crimes. Justice would see to that. And along the way he would uncover his identity and the truth of his past.

Because that was the only way he might pursue the life he wanted with Nora and Eli.

CHAPTER 41

Nora choked up when she saw the new house. Eli followed her from room to room, gaping at everything with disbelief.

It was a wonderful moment for Justice. The house didn't surprise him, of course. He'd been overseeing its construction.

"Oh Justice," Nora said, giving his hand a squeeze, "I can't believe it's really ours."

The house had three bedrooms, a nice kitchen, and a cold room. The barn and stable were triple the size of their predecessors. They'd built the new bunkhouse in the shade of a large cottonwood. Any day now, they'd start construction of a new, much larger smokehouse.

Nora had planned the house, but this was her first time seeing it, since she and Eli had stayed in Santa Fe helping Mary with her new baby, a healthy little girl she'd name Nora Colette.

Justice had hired two old hands, Pedro Martin and Silas Sutton, to help with the 135 head of cattle Nora would now be running on her ground and the new 2000-acre parcel

Justice had tacked onto her land. He liked and trusted both men and made sure they had everything they needed.

Nora had good forage on her land and, of course, plenty of river frontage, but she was still thinking of selling off 20 or 30 head. She shared Pedro's concern that her current herd was too large for the acreage. In this country drought was never far away.

Justice had cut out the best bull and finest half dozen cows from the 124 head the association had insisted on giving him. These he added to Nora's herd. Then he sold his remaining cattle and deposited $2500 of the resulting $3000. Along with the money Nora had left over, the cash she made selling some cows, and the $2000 bounty Justice had earned for bagging Del Mundo, this took their joint account to almost $7000.

Justice would take the remaining $500 he'd earned selling cows with him to Leadville.

He would miss Nora and Eli. He'd miss Dagger, too, and Rafer.

Over the last several weeks Justice had spent a great deal of time riding the steel dust stallion. They ranged across the ranch together, often followed by the panting shadow of the loyal and formidable Rafer.

Never had he known such a horse. Riding Dagger was like riding the wind itself, flying across the scrub at unfathomable speeds. The horse was faster than any he'd ever ridden, any he'd ever seen, and had great endurance to boot.

For several days after moving into the new house, Nora was a whirlwind, making the home her own, filling it with furniture and fixtures, from curtains to corner cabinets, exerting that feminine touch that makes a house a home.

Justice was impressed.

Nora had enough money now to pack the place from wall to wall with whatever she wanted, but the house had a bright, uncluttered charm. She added touches of color here and there in the form of flowers, paintings, and pottery. On the white wall behind her heavy farmhouse table, she hung a particularly beautiful red and gold horse blanket.

As much as he hated to leave, Justice knew it was time.

Nora knew it, too.

The first night after Justice slept in the spare bedroom, she prepared a splendid breakfast of bacon, fried potatoes and onions, toast, and jam.

After breakfast Nora helped him pack his things. He had his Colt, of course. He also brought an extra Peacemaker, a .44 caliber Webley bulldog pocket pistol he'd appropriated during the raid on Tucker's ranch house, and extra ammunition for all his weapons. He also carried the big Bowie knife, a shaving kit, and clothes, including a heavy sheepskin jacket lined with wool.

Harvest time was mostly behind them here in the valley. Nights were getting cold. Up in Leadville nights would already be dropping below freezing.

He'd be taking the train, of course, but he planned on searching the big boomtown from one end to another until he found Cochran, learned what he needed to learn, and did what he had to do.

When it was time to leave he got Dagger ready and told Pedro to saddle up. The old ranch hand would ride with him to Dos Pesos, then bring back Dagger on a lead. Pedro would also see that Dagger and the other horses had plenty of exercise while Justice was away.

When Justice saw Rafer he looked the dog in the eye and said, "Anybody messes with the family, rip their throats out, you hear me?"

Then Justice called to Eli, pulled him aside, and gave him his pocketknife.

"Gee, thanks, Justice," the boy said, marveling over the

knife he'd watched Justice use so many times and so many ways.

"You're welcome, son. A man needs a good pocketknife. You keep that with you all the time and be careful whenever you use it. Your mama will have my hide if you cut yourself."

Eli laughed. "Yes sir."

"I know you can handle it. That's why I'm giving it to you in the first place. While I'm away you're gonna be the man of the house, you understand?"

"Yes sir."

"I'm counting on you to take good care of your mother. You listen to her, and you look out for her, all right?"

The boy stood a little straighter. "Yes sir. You can count on me."

"I know I can, son. I care very deeply about you and your mother, so you take care of yourself, too, okay?"

Eli nodded. "Justice, will you come back?"

"I will."

"My daddy never came back."

"I know, son. I'm sorry about that."

"I just hope you will come back."

"I will, Eli. That is a promise."

Eli grinned brightly. "That's good, Justice. When you come back, will you teach me to shoot like you shoot?"

Justice mussed the boy's straw-colored hair. "I sure will, son. I sure will."

They ambled together over to Nora, who told Eli to go feed the chickens.

"He's going to miss you," she told Justice.

"I'm going to miss him."

"I wish you didn't have to go."

"I wish the same thing."

"I know." She slid her hands into his. "Please come back to us."

"I will. I promise you that."

"Don't go getting shot."

"Well, that I can't promise. But I will return to you one way or the other."

Nora took a deep breath and looked away across the ranch, blinking. He knew she was having a hard time. Her eyes seeped tears, but she was too tough to sob.

"Thank you," he said. "For everything."

She nodded, sniffing. "The same to you. Thank you... for everything." She gave his hands a squeeze.

He'd never wanted so badly to kiss someone in his whole life and felt confident that that went for his old life, too.

"All right, then," he said, his voice thick with emotion. "I reckon I'd best get on down the road."

"Justice, wait," Nora said, squeezing his hands again and piercing his eyes with her sky-blue gaze. "I need to talk to you, to tell you..."

"I'll be back," he said. "You don't have to—"

"Yes, I do. Justice, I love you."

He smiled at her. "I love you, too, Nora."

"I love you," she said again, "and I want you to come back. Not just for a visit, Justice, do you understand? Not just as a friend. I want to marry you. I want to live our lives together. I want you to be Eli's father and raise him up to be the man he could be with you in his life. I want more children. Your babies, Justice. I want to fill this house, then kick myself for not building a bigger place." She laughed but lifted her eyes skyward and blinked away tears. "I'm sorry. I know this is forward of me, and I don't mean to make you uncomfortable, and I hope I don't scare you off, but before you left, I had to—"

He crushed her to him in a loving embrace. "I want all these things, too, Nora. All of them. I want you to be my wife and the mother of my children, including Eli. I want to watch him grow up to be a good man, and I want to grow old with you, staring into those beautiful blue eyes of yours until the day I die. That's why I'm leaving, okay? Not just to find Cochran and set things right, not just to figure out who I was, but to make sure I'm clear and free to live the life I want to live with you."

"Can't we just forget about the past?" she cried. "Can't we both just start over... together?"

"No, we can't, darlin." He leaned forward and kissed her forehead. It was the first time either of them had kissed the other. He wanted more, wanted so much more, but this would have to do for now. "I love you and Eli too much to do that. I'm going to go sort out my past, and once that's done, I'll ride back to you. And Nora, I pray that when I do, I can sweep you into my arms and give you the kiss I've been dying to give you."

"There is nothing in the whole world I would love more than that, Justice."

"Likewise. Because if that comes to pass, you'll know that it is forever."

———

THANK YOU FOR READING *A MAN CALLED JUSTICE*.

Justice's adventures continue in *Justice Returns*.

If you enjoyed this story, <u>please be a friend and leave a review</u>. When you leave even a short review, you just bought my family dinner, because Amazon will show the book to more people. I sure would appreciate your help.

If you enjoyed the book but don't have time to review, please consider leaving a 5-star rating. It's quick and simple and helps me get this new series off the ground.

I love Westerns and hope to bring you 8 or 10 a year. To

hear about new releases, special sales, and giveaways, <u>join my reader list</u>.

Once more, thanks for reading. I hope our paths cross again.

Until then, don't approach a bull from the front, a horse from the rear, or a fool from any direction.

ABOUT THE AUTHOR

I was born six months before man landed on the moon and lucky enough to grow up in the country, where my family lived largely off the land.

When I wasn't fishing, exploring the woods, or weeding the garden, I devoured comic books like *Two-Gun Kid* and *The Rawhide Kid* before moving on to the exciting adventure stories of Jack London and Louis L'Amour.

Our black-and-white TV only got three channels, though you could lose one and pick up another if you went outside and messed with the antenna. On its grainy screen, we watched *Gunsmoke*, *Bonanza*, and movies starring John Wayne and Clint Eastwood.

Now a husband and father, I love traveling the West and reading history and fiction alike. My favorite authors are Louis L'Amour, Elmore Leonard, C.J. Petit, and R.O. Lane.

As a writer, I hope to entertain you with fun stories of the old West. My good guys are good, my bad guys are bad, and you'll always find a touch of romance to sweeten the grit.

If you'd like to keep in touch, join my newsletter HERE.

ALSO BY JOHN DEACON

A Man Called Justice (Silent Justice #1)

Justice Returns (Silent Justice #2)

Final Justice (Silent Justice #3)

Justice Rides Again (Silent Justice #4)

Destitution

Heck's Journey (Heck & Hope #1)

Heck's Valley (Heck & Hope #2)

Heck's Gold (Heck & Hope #3)

Heck's Gamble (Heck & Hope #4)

Heck's Stand (Heck & Hope #5)

Made in the USA
Las Vegas, NV
05 April 2024

88296795R00135